MW00416748

THE DREDGE

THE DREDGE

A NOVEL

BRENDAN FLAHERTY

Atlantic Monthly Press
New York

FIRST EDITION

Published simultaneously in Canada
Printed in the United States of America

First Grove Atlantic hardcover edition: March 2024

This book was set in 12-pt. Bembo
by Alpha Design & Composition of Pittsfield, NH.

Library of Congress Cataloging-in-Publication data is available for this title.

ISBN 978-0-8021-6256-4
eISBN 978-0-8021-6257-1

Atlantic Monthly Press
an imprint of Grove Atlantic
154 West 14th Street
New York, NY 10011

Distributed by Publishers Group West

groveatlantic.com

24 25 26 27 10 9 8 7 6 5 4 3 2 1

For my family
& in memory of James T. Flaherty

Come down off the cross
We can use the wood
—Tom Waits

I

1

Some families are haunted. The stuff of the past, the traumas and ghosts—they just go on and on, Cale Casey felt as he crossed the white marble floor of his bedroom. He passed through white curtains to the balcony, where he slumped to the rail. The Pacific heaved and shimmered in the moonlight like a sheet of hammered nickel, and the surf yawned on the beach beneath the bluff. He took the cell phone from his sweatpants pocket to check the time again. Midnight in Honolulu, it was now the first of March, the month of his darkest memories. And he remembered a moment nearly thirty years before, on the worst day of his life, when he was fourteen and coming home through icy woods with his younger brother, Ambrose.

"Don't fall."

He spooked and turned to see Janelle stepping onto the balcony through the open sliding doors. She wore one of his undershirts, which fell well above her knees. Her smile faded. "You okay, Reese?"

That was his middle name, his professional name. What he went by now. Just about everyone he'd known back in Macoun, Connecticut, had called him Cale, short for Caleb, but he hadn't been there in a long time and he had no plans of ever going back.

"Didn't mean to wake you," he said.

"You look like you saw an *I don't know what*." She stood beside him. A warm wind bearing the sweet lemon scent of plumeria pushed her long black hair away from her face. The curtains flagged into the bedroom. The flapping streaks of white.

"Maybe I did," he said.

"You're shivering."

"Caught a chill."

She bumped him with her hip. "I thought haole blood was supposed to be thicker."

"Guess it thins out over ten years."

"You want a shirt?"

He gripped the rail and shook his head no.

"You feel sick?"

"Yes." He cleared his throat. "But that's not it."

She tilted her head, studying him. "Did I say too much tonight?"

They'd been seeing each other for two months. At dinner that evening, she'd mentioned marriage and kids.

For the first time, those ideas had filled him with excitement instead of the urge to run.

"No," he said. "The opposite."

"Good, I wasn't sure. You got pretty quiet after that."

"Sorry."

"No need for sorries," she said. "I just know what I'm looking for, you know, and I'm too old to waste my time anymore."

"What are you again anyway, eighteen?" He noticed that talking to her made him feel steady again.

"Shut up."

"Nineteen?"

"I'm not saying it has to be tomorrow," she said. "But."

He laughed, distracted. "Got it."

She tapped his chest with her pointer finger. "I'll tell you the truth, though."

"What's that now?"

"The jury's still out on you," she said. "I know the judge pretty well, but she does have some lingering questions about you, if we're being honest."

"Oh yeah, like what?"

"Like, who are you?"

He laughed again, this time thinking she was messing with him.

"I phrased that weird," she said. "But I mean it."

"Who am I?" He looked at her. "That's what you're asking?"

"Yes."

He thought about that. "Well, I'm a guy, I think. Forty-three years old. Gemini. Sunsets, if you must know."

"Reese," she said. "This is what you do."

"One of the best, I'd say probably *the* best realtor on Oahu. No offense."

"All you talk about is work."

"I bore you?"

"Occasionally you mention surfing and golf. I know you like music."

"And smoothies too. Don't forget smoothies."

"How profound." She slapped the rail. "How brave of you, sir, to share such a deep part of your twisted soul."

He turned to her and lifted her chin with his thumb. "I like you. I ask about you."

"Especially when I ask about you."

"Why do you think that is?" He smiled at her.

She shook her head. "You may think that's cute, but I think you're just trying to get around saying anything real."

He stood up straight and scratched his head. "I don't know what you want me to say."

She put her hand on his shoulder. "I feel like I know you, but also that I don't really know you at all."

He nodded slightly. "I've heard that before."

Her hand dropped. "Well, I find that strange. And it worries me."

"Why?"

"Because I like you, you idiot," she said. "A lot, obviously. But also, I'm afraid you have secrets."

"Everyone has secrets."

"So, tell me one."

"Well." He leaned on the rail again. "I wet the bed until I was in fifth grade."

"Ew. That's not what I had in mind."

"It's true, and now I'm embarrassed. Happy? Was that real enough for you?"

"Isn't that like one of the early signs that someone's a serial killer?"

His eyes shifted away. With her, he felt a stronger romantic potential than any he'd ever known in his adult life. But he realized in that moment that of course it wouldn't work out. Because he was doomed. Unworthy of love.

"I'm going to get some water," she said. "I want you to think of something better for when I get back."

"It's your turn now."

"You thirsty?"

"No, thanks."

"Yeah, you'd better not." She laughed.

He came back into the bedroom as she walked off through the big house, brand new in every detail. The sound of her bare feet slapping the hallway's polished concrete floor receded from him.

"I'm sorry," he whispered, thinking of a girl named Lily from his childhood, as the memory of his brother in the woods returned.

He could see it all so clearly still. He and Ambrose were on their way back from Gibbs Pond as the first flurries fell in what was known in their little part of northern Connecticut as the No Name Storm. Caused by two nor'easters colliding, it buried the country from Alabama to Maine in March of 1993. That day, as they stepped into the field beside their house at last, they saw Harvey Gindewin's police cruiser in the driveway. And Cale knew in an instant that their family was finished.

2

Ambrose Casey stepped off the porch of his childhood home into a warm fog before dawn. His right boot crunched in what was left of the snow he'd pulled off the roof. It'd been through a few cycles since, of melting and freezing again. March. The rest of the lawn was yellowy brown and wet, and he walked across a path of bluestone slabs to a white truck that read *Casey Homes* on the doors in black script. It was almost a replica of his father's.

His wife, Kate, eight months pregnant with their second child, stood on the porch holding their first. Sadie waved goodbye to her daddy. Her fingers opened and folded to her palm like eyelashes blinking. He blew a kiss and smoothed his beard. Reaching for the door handle, he paused and then returned to his family. He laid his palm upon his unborn boy and kissed his daughter again.

"Love you, Sadie," he said.

"I want cookie, Da-da."

"Da-da wants cookie too." He eyed his wife.

"Nope." Kate shook her head. "Da-da's been a real bad boy."

"You have no idea." He smiled and went away in the truck. Down Apple Brook Road, the same way his daddy had. He coasted down the hill and then passed a big rising pasture where, a couple years back, a few dozen cows had been replaced by three horses. A banker from New York had bought the place for his wife's show ponies.

Ambrose drove over the short bridge spanning Flash Brook. In the woods, a quarter mile south of the road, Flash Brook met Fox Brook. There, the rushing waters stilled in the shadows of high crags at a pool people called Gibbs Pond. The Gibbs family had harvested ice there and sold it from the back of mule-drawn wagons in the days before refrigeration. Even in the dead of summer, the pool was about twenty feet deep, to a bottom of thick silt that turned the Coca-Cola-colored water to chocolate milk in the muddy surge of the thaw.

In a year with heavy snows and a sudden spring, the water spread over the banks and covered the little valley it'd carved there long ago. It papered dead leaves high up the trunks of the pines and maples, and pulled along with it the loosely rooted saplings and rotted limbs into the larger Apple Brook, which fed the Farmington River like a root, which built the trunk of the Connecticut River, which bloomed into the Sound, the Atlantic. Oceans everywhere, blood of earth.

Ambrose passed the old guesthouse the Gibbses had operated briefly as a bed-and-breakfast, and then their main house, which was older than all the country's declared wars. He'd last seen Meryl Gibbs in January, when he'd come to snowplow. She'd called before Christmas to thank him and let him know that she was going to visit her son in Florida for the rest of the winter. But backing out that day, he saw a downstairs curtain stir. Through a strip of glass, as fogged as a cataract, there she was, skeletal and obscure. She raised her hand and then the window filled with the darkness of empty space, and the curtain dropped back over it. He didn't play the radio for the rest of that day. He carried on in silence with the image of the old woman in the glass looping in his mind and radiating out a soft humming pain through the hairs of his body. Each one a transmitter.

Meryl Gibbs had said many times over the years that when she died, her property would go to the town land trust. She didn't want it stripped for topsoil and littered with McMansions. Ambrose always hoped that she'd live long enough for him to buy it from her. It was a beautiful piece of nature, anyone who'd seen it knew, and he'd known it since before he could remember. Sadie knew it too. He and Kate had hiked there during both pregnancies.

But Ambrose's money wasn't pouring in. To make more, and to build houses of the highest quality, he'd started his own company. It was more expensive than he'd planned, and the demand was lower than he'd hoped. People here, he found, generally appreciated the craftsmanship, but they didn't want to pay more for less house. In his second year in business, the coronavirus pandemic didn't help. Sellers of existing structures and high-velocity builders had made more money than ever. But for Ambrose, the materials he needed were harder to get and more expensive. The workers he'd brought in on jobs before were not interested anymore. They were either hunkered down or earning more with bigger companies. And he was increasingly concerned about his business going belly-up. Baby at home, baby on the way.

Still, he continued to keep an eye on the Gibbs place, including plowing for free, which he'd been doing since he was sixteen. He did it, he said, for the privilege of fishing Gibbs Pond, though he hadn't fished at all in three decades now, since a golden afternoon in September 1992, when he'd just started in the seventh grade.

That day, he'd long believed, was the beginning of all the trouble with the Rowes. The day he'd sat there on that mossy bank with his brother, Cale, listening to their father tell them finally how their grandmother disappeared.

3

Lily Rowe got an email Monday morning that ruined her week. Her boss wanted her to go to the office instead of the jobsite for a meeting Tuesday afternoon. He had a matter of high importance to discuss. His name was Frank Gerlano, and he was the CEO of Valley Development Corp. Lily had had no contact with him in more than three months, since she'd been named the 2021 employee of the year at the company holiday dinner. At the dinner, Gerlano gave a toast in the banquet hall at the Inn in Nevin, the town south of Macoun, in front of a hundred people, almost all men. He praised Lily's intelligence and work ethic.

"This girl's a real workaholic," he said, "and I mean that as a compliment. Nothing outside of work ever gets in her way, no distractions."

The girl was forty-one years old. She was single, they all knew, and always had been, people said. And she still lived alone up on Waquaheag Road, in the house that her family had occupied since they first drifted into Macoun, when she was in the sixth grade. The house had belonged to a local farmer named Seb Bainer, who'd inherited it from his brother, Bob, after Bob flipped a tractor. Seb had put a handwritten flyer advertising it for rent on the corkboard in the general store, under the thumbtacked business cards of plumbers and offerings of old lawn mowers and used dogs. By chance it caught the eye of Lily's father, whose need for more beer resulted in a fateful pit stop.

He was tired after six hours behind the wheel, so he drove up to Seb's place in the family pickup, with his wife sitting shotgun and his two kids still lying in the truck bed under a tied-down tarp. Old Seb took pity on Lily and Ray shaking in his driveway, and he agreed that the Rowes could rent his dead brother's house month to month, though it gave him a sick feeling in the pit of his stomach, he admitted afterward to Harvey Gindewin. Later, a town gossip down at the Fish House bar said that Seb must've had designs all along on Lily's mother, Bonnie Rowe, who could've been a beauty in another life. The accusation was that Seb's lust was the crack where the weed took root. That was more false than it was true, Lily knew, but the Rowes had been given shelter nevertheless.

As a teenager, Lily learned how to fix up that house herself, with the help of a library card, and that was how she'd cut her teeth in construction. She had a natural talent for it, it turned out. That led to something of a passion and, in time, to her role as a project superintendent with Valley, the biggest developer in the county. There, her employee of the year award was tangible proof that she'd risen.

"So, let's all raise a glass to Lily Rowe," Gerlano announced to the banquet hall. "She's doing a killer job at the Nevin Village Residential Shoppes, which are, thanks to her, ahead of schedule." He invited her up front to accept a commemorative glass plaque and a gift certificate for three hundred dollars to La Ristorante. She was one of a handful of people there wearing a medical mask, though she'd been vaccinated against Covid. The number of cases was surging in the state again then, just in time for the winter holidays, but people were sick of it. She wondered if they could tell she was blushing as she rested her chin in her hands, with her elbows propped on the red-clothed round table.

"Go on up there," said a bald machine operator seated across from her. "Go on up and get your prize."

She began threading her way to the front of the room, with a hesitant yet athletic grace. She wore black flats and a black sleeveless dress with pockets, no jewelry, no purse, nothing extra. The crowd clapped, a few whistles.

"Way to go, Josey!" a voice called out, and some laughed and clapped harder. Josey was a nickname a demolition crew had given her, a nod to a Clint Eastwood cowboy character, the old strong, silent type. They said Lily didn't have to say much to say a lot. But privately, Gerlano had advised her that it wouldn't hurt if she talked more, smiled more. "Don't cancel me for telling you the truth," he'd said. "But act happy. It's good for business."

She shook his hand and took the plaque and gift certificate with a simple "Thanks."

He said, "How about a few words?"

"I don't think so," she told him quietly. "I'm not much of a public speaker."

"Come on," he said. He'd been known to drink waters disguised as martinis while buying the real thing for potential business partners. And he'd also been known to have two too many Scotches at his company parties and make an offhand remark that rankled someone thereafter. He looked at Lily and raised his glass of amber. "Don't be shy now."

"Speech!" someone called out, and then, like howler monkeys, many of them: "Speech! Speech!"

She took a deep breath. "I don't have much to say," she said, without removing her mask. She'd actually grown to like wearing it. She always hated the way she looked anyway. Her features too often reminded her of her parents'.

"You could dedicate your award to somebody?" Gerlano suggested. "A boyfriend?"

She looked at him.

He tugged at his collar in mock discomfort. "Noted," he said, drawing some laughs. "Your mother then? Everybody has a mother, right?"

There were a few soft groans amid the crowd. Many in the room knew already that her mother had died by suicide. Several even knew that, when Lily was eighteen, Bonnie Rowe had wound up on Seb Bainer's kitchen floor, gurgling foam and blood, after drinking drain cleaner.

Gerlano was from elsewhere, though. He'd come from White Plains, New York, only four years before, seeking opportunity and a less competitive market, and he'd found both. She wondered for a moment if he'd made that remark intentionally to embarrass her in some kind of warped psychological gamesmanship, or if he was just jabbering in front of the crowd with his Scotch. It seemed unlikely that he didn't know the public facts of her history. She knew how he operated, which she planned to use against him someday. Someday, she'd be rich, richer than him. She'd be the big boss who never got toyed with like some powerless thing, and she'd find a way to really fuck him up.

Lily turned and faced the crowd. She felt faint and her vision grayed, obscuring their faces into a swath of dim and blurry smudges. She cleared her throat. "People say everybody gets a trophy now, but this is the first one I've ever gotten. So thanks, I guess?" She looked at the little glass plaque. "If you think I should dedicate it to someone, Frank, then I dedicate it to my big brother, Ray. When I was little, he was my protector. He had his problems, but he was always loyal. And when people pushed him, eventually he pushed back, harder." She glanced at her boss. "That's it. Thanks."

She heard whispers at a nearby table, and she assumed they were talking about Ray. People had said he was crazy and dangerous, though only she knew how he'd suffered. He'd run away when he was fifteen, slipped out at a smart time, without telling her goodbye. And she was still waiting for him to come back.

She didn't look toward the whispers as she passed with her awards. She took her black leather jacket off the back of her chair and left the plaque at the table where she'd been sitting. And though the buffet hadn't opened yet, she walked out, hoping no one was watching.

4

The morning Cale broke up with Janelle, he stared out at the golf course from his office at Ono Real Estate, thinking of something his father once told him and his brother. He said, "The great flood of 1955 killed two hundred people in Connecticut, but only one was from Macoun, and she was my mother."

They were all sitting together on the bank of Gibbs Pond. It was a Sunday, they'd been to church that morning, early September 1992. The heat of summer had only just been tempered by the cool edge of fall. The leaves on the maples and oaks were still green, though they'd grown stiff and lacked the suppleness of spring.

Cale, who'd turned fourteen over that summer, had just started in the eighth grade. He was thin and slight still. A late bloomer, the pediatrician said. He wore a Hartford Whalers hockey t-shirt and black nylon soccer shorts, and he sat cross-legged on the bank, barefoot, holding his fishing pole straight up with both hands.

Almost thirteen, Ambrose was already an inch taller and more solid than his older brother. He had his father's blue eyes and strong chin, people said. He wore a baseball cap over thick brown hair and he'd taken off his t-shirt. The mosquitoes and gnats had begun relenting finally, thanks to the lower temperatures at night. A yellow dog, a one-year-old Labrador mix named Sammy, lay curled up beside him on the bank in a beam of sunlight.

Their father, Eli, ran a coarse hand through his short dark hair, which was only a little silver on the sides. Strong and trim, he still fit easily into the Navy uniform he'd worn at eighteen.

He went on to tell the boys that their grandmother had been arguing, hissing whispers in the bedroom with his father, who'd left a door open to the pounding rain when he came in from the barn, where the known secret was he kept a coffee can filled with gin amid the coffee cans filled with screws. After the argument, she came into the den, where little Eli was pushing a toy truck along the scuffed plank floor. She lifted him in a hug and carried him to the living room, where she wrapped him in a knit blanket on the sofa. On the table beside him, she put a bottle of Schweppes ginger ale, a Kid Colt comic, and two Matchbox cars to go along with the truck. She pressed her cool palm against his forehead and told him she was going down to Fox Brook to notch the high-water mark on one of the trees there.

"Why?" their father had asked, as a child.

"For history," she said. "To remind us. When the storm's over."

"I want to go with you."

"No, we need you to get better."

"I don't want to stay here."

"You'll be safer here. Daddy's asleep anyway."

"Please."

"I'll be right back. I just need a moment to myself, okay?"

When he heard her leave through the back door, he went to the kitchen window and waited. The panes rattled in their frames, whipped by the wind. That was the second hurricane that week, and it'd turned all the land into a sponge that could hold no more. Through the water streaming down the window glass, he saw his mother cross the field beside the house, under a granite sky. The tall grass all around her was bent and slumped. The sucking earth pulled at her black rubber boots, every step. On the edge of the woods, she looked back at the house. Her long dark hair slicked down. The big gabardine raincoat her husband had worn as an Allied soldier in the forests of Belgium clung to her, soaked through already. She held up her hand. It would've been impossible for her to see her son in the window under the eaves, but he waved back with all his might. And then she stepped onto the path and she was gone.

As the story concluded, Cale looked at his father, stunned, mouth agape.

"You can still see the high water mark she carved that day," his dad said, setting down his fishing pole on the bank. "Last I checked, that cedar still stands, about a mile up the brook."

"Our grandma carved that tree?" asked Cale. "I've seen that. Why didn't you tell us?"

"Telling you now." Their father picked up his pole and reeled in his line slowly. "Maybe I should've told you sooner so you'd know why you need to be careful around water. Or maybe I shouldn't have burdened you with it at all, though, right?" The red-and-white plastic fishing bobber dragged across the smooth surface. "Today's her birthday is why it probably popped in my head."

"So she drowned?" asked Ambrose. "Behind our house? Grandma drowned? That's what happened?"

"Yes," his father said. "Seems yes."

"Seems?" Cale asked. "They didn't find her?"

"No."

"Maybe she just ran away, then?"

Their father spit. "Probably not."

"Why not?" Ambrose asked.

His father tucked his lightweight gray flannel shirt into his blue jeans. "I don't know."

Whatever else might've been said about their grandmother that day was interrupted by a stone falling from the ledge and thunking into the water.

"Was that a fish?" Cale whispered. His dad shook his head and looked up as another stone, a bigger one, a rock, knocked off a tree behind them and landed in the leaf litter.

"Hello?" Cale called out. Another rock came down, this one missing him by a few feet. "Hey, who's up there?"

"Hey, fuck you," responded a voice, a teenage boy. Cale couldn't see him through all the trees, but he knew immediately it was Ray Rowe.

"Watch your mouth," Cale's dad shouted. "Stop with the rocks. You can hurt someone." A whooshing sound came through the trees and then a metal-shafted arrow thumped into the bank they stood on. It vibrated, ten feet from where Ambrose sat.

"That could've killed me." Ambrose stood up quickly.

"Get out of here." Ray laughed, an exaggerated cackle. "This place is mine now."

The Caseys reeled in their lines. "You boys go," their father commanded them, and Cale and Ambrose hurried away from the water, their lines wrapping around the poles, bobbers knocking. They went over a rise, the dog in the lead, and they didn't stop until the edge of the pasture. Their dad met them there a minute later. "You know who that was?" he asked them.

"Ray Rowe," Cale said. "He's on our bus."

"So that's that Abe Rowe's son, then?"

"He's a psychopath. People say he eats rats."

"Well, you don't say that. But I'm going to let Chief Gindewin know about what happened today."

"You're gonna get him arrested?" Cale said.

"I didn't say that, but you can't be shooting arrows at people. That's a threat and a danger. Is this kid out of his mind? And he's trespassing too. I've been fishing that hole my entire life with Meryl's permission, and some kid thinks he's gonna run me off now?"

"Don't," Cale said. "He'll just be back on the bus and he'll know we snitched."

His father looked at him and sighed. "You guys stay away from him, okay?"

"That's gonna be hard for Cale." Ambrose smirked. "He has a crush on Ray's dirty little sister, Lily."

"I do not."

"I saw you staring at plain Jane at the general store. There she was in her ripped sweatpants, buying baloney, and you were drooling like a Saint Bernard."

"You shut your mouth, Am."

"Or what?"

"Boys!" their father snapped. "Enough. You don't know how lucky you are to have each other."

Ambrose kicked a stone in the dirt and grumbled, "Well, I'm not afraid of Ray Rowe."

"Maybe you should be," Cale said.

Ambrose glared at him. They were friends who'd spent whole summers playing Wiffle ball together, frogging, building forts. But now that they were in the same school, on the same bus, the same soccer team, Ambrose had begun to question the old hierarchies of age. Their personalities, in the midst of their own changes, had begun to grate against one another.

Ambrose said, "We can't all be cowards, Cale."

"We can't all be stupid hotheads either, Am."

"I said, enough," their father said. "You need to have each another's backs no matter what, you hear me?"

It was something he'd told them often. But later, well into adulthood, Cale thought that perhaps his father had somehow sensed what was coming even then. And he wondered if that day was truly the beginning of the end. Or if it went back further, to the flood when his father was a boy, and back to a war before that boy was born, and back and back and back.

5

Ambrose stood at the kitchen sink, scrubbing chicken fibers from the cast-iron pan. Night, and the windows were mirrors. His reflection moved amid the objects of his life, dishes and refrigerator magnets. He could hear Kate in the living room, reading to Sadie. Not the words exactly, but the smooth steady sound of her voice. At dinner, she'd suggested some names for the new baby, including Ambrose, a junior, which he rejected.

"Fine with me," she said. "I thought you'd be flattered."

"He'll inherit enough of my garbage."

She reached for the dish of green beans he'd sauteed in garlic butter. "I just want him to be a good man like you."

"Am I?" He laughed, watching Sadie push a potato through a puddle of water on her highchair tray. Her plastic cup was on its side. She spilled it on purpose so often that they just gave her an inch of water at a time.

"Some people seem to think so," Kate said.

"They're probably right."

"Yeah, the crowd never makes mistakes," she said. "But for the name, I guess we'll just go with 'Ronald,' then."

He marveled. "Ah, such beauty."

"Ronald Reagan McDonald Casey," she said.

He lifted his chin and took a breath, as if he were inhaling fresh mountain air. "That's got a nice ring to it, doesn't it?"

"A born champion," she agreed.

"Actor, fast-food clown, billionaire."

"You could do a lot worse for yourself." She dropped a cloth napkin on Sadie's tray puddle. "What about 'Abraham'?"

He looked at her, all lightheartedness snuffed out. "That's a joke?"

She laughed. "It was my grandpa's middle name. I kinda like it. It's classic. Abe."

"Absolutely not." His response was too curt. She eyed him skeptically but was distracted by Sadie suggesting the baby be named "Doggie." Ambrose left the table.

"We're going with Doggie," Kate called after him.

"Ha," he responded, passing through the living room.

"Where are you going?"

"Bathroom," he said, but he went out to the garage and paced the floor. He grabbed a beer from an unrefrigerated twelve-pack. The can was cool, but not cold. He popped it open and the beer foamed over his fingers. He drank it quickly.

It was the second warm day in a row, and the birds outside were still tittering in the twilight with a spring fervor, though it'd begun to drizzle. When he came back into the kitchen, Kate was putting things in the fridge.

"I got this." He squeezed between her and the counter. "Your feet are probably killing you."

"Why do you smell like beer?" she said.

"I had a beer."

"Where?"

"I don't know," he said, in a way that meant: no more questions.

"Okay, guy, check yourself," she said. "Let's go read a book, Sadie. Dad wants to clean up all by himself."

Ambrose finished scrubbing the cast-iron pan and dried it with a white dish towel. He put the pan in the drying rack beside the sink and went to the living room, where he leaned against the doorjamb.

"Sorry," he said.

"What's going on with you?" She laid the book down on her knee.

"I don't know. Work?"

"We're gonna be fine, okay? This pandemic bull s-h-i-t is going to lift. It already is, and things will level out."

He scratched his head. "Maybe it's just March?"

She nodded. "I get it."

"Do you?" He tried to chuckle, but it sounded thin.

"I'm trying to," she said. "I've been trying to for how many years?"

"I know. You do get it. You do."

"Maybe I don't," she said. "So, why don't you tell me, then?" Sadie took the book from Kate and flipped through the pages, humming.

"There's nothing to say," he said. "It's nothing."

"Then I can't help," she said. "But your moodiness lately is not my favorite."

"Look. You want to know why I don't like the name Abe?"

She laughed. "Relax. That one's off the table. I was half kidding anyway."

"There used to be a guy in town named Abe." Ambrose sat down on the couch beside her. Then he told her about Abe Rowe, and what happened just a few weeks after Ray Rowe shot his arrow at them at Gibbs Pond.

That day, Ambrose remembered, his dad was driving them to the hardware store. On the way, they passed the Fish House, a little restaurant that had the only bar in Macoun. And right in front, they saw a big guy bent over, pulling a woman by the wrists across the gravel parking lot, her heels dragging.

Ambrose's dad slowed and then quickly pulled into the lot. He opened the truck door and put one foot down on the gravel. "Everything okay?"

The man had wild long gray hair falling down over his face. He released the woman and stood up straighter, pushing his hair back. Even from that distance, Ambrose could see his eyes were pale and the whites red. His face was bloated, ragged. The woman sat on the ground, shaking her head no, no, no. Her green sweatshirt had a wet stain down the belly, a spilled drink, it looked like.

"We're fine," the big man said, his voice a coarse croak. "You?"

"You sure?"

"Run along now, boy, if you know what's good for you."

Eli Casey got out of the truck and slammed the door shut. "You okay, ma'am?"

The woman nodded now, yes, yes, yes.

"I don't think we've met yet, Abe. But I know of you already."

"Well, if I wanted to hear from an asshole, I'd fart," he said.

"Whatever that means."

"It means I'm calling you an asshole. A stinky little asshole."

"Says the guy dragging a woman across a parking lot."

"I'll do what I want with my wife."

"The law might disagree," Eli said.

"The law ain't here."

"Yeah, but I am."

Abe wiped his nose with the back of his hand. "Nothing you can do about nothing."

"I think even you can understand that right now that's not true."

"You think you're a good guy, eh?" Abe took a step closer. "Well, you're not."

"I didn't say I was."

Through the windshield, Ambrose saw Abe stare at him, a dead look in his eye.

"That your little toy?" Abe smiled and flicked his head toward Ambrose. "It sure is a good-looking boy you got there."

"You're about one second from getting put down like a rabid dog." Eli's voice was low, steady.

"You hear that, Bonnie? Let's get out of here before this turd tries to get the cops to shit all over us again."

Ambrose saw his dad take a step toward them and say, "Cops have nothing to do with this right here."

Bonnie got up. "My hero," she squealed, in mock relief. "All my problems are solved. Thank God for the law."

Abe laughed, mocking, an exaggerated cackle that reminded Ambrose of the way Ray had laughed the day he ran them off from Gibbs Pond.

Ambrose's dad said, "So you're both just piss drunk then, is it?"

"Free country," Abe said. "Mind your own damn business."

"Well, I see where your son gets it."

"You have no idea." Abe took Bonnie by the elbow, but she ripped her arm away and became suddenly sincere.

"Thank you for your concern. No one cares about us. Thank you."

Eli cocked his head, clearly confused by this sudden and severe shift in tone. Abe turned toward his truck and flipped his middle finger, holding it over his head. Bonnie followed him, walking backward, her hands pressed together as if in prayer, bowing, mouthing the words, over and over, "Thank you."

"Some people," Ambrose's father said as he watched Abe and Bonnie slowly stumble away. He got back in the truck.

"He called you an asshole," Ambrose said.

"I've been called worse." He put it in reverse and turned around.

"He called you worse."

"Some people really believe they have nothing to lose. Those are dangerous people, son. Those are crazy people."

"I'm madder than you are." Ambrose turned in his seat to look back at the Rowes.

"I don't think so, son." His father kept watching in the rearview. "But some day you may have children of your own, and you'll understand. You gotta weigh your risks, because the consequences are more than just yours. In a way, that man reminds me of a worse version of my dad. How would you like a father like that?"

Ambrose faced forward, disappointed, feeling sick in his stomach.

"This guy's really going to drive like this now, and wreck somebody else?" his dad shook his head.

"Let's just go already," Ambrose said.

"I'm about to be a bad example." His dad put the truck in park again. "This is stupid." He got out and walked over to the Rowes' truck. He gave a polite wave. Ambrose could see Abe sitting straight up in his seat. He saw his father approach the driver-side window and then he saw him reach in and pull the keys out. They glinted in the sunlight before he dropped them in the truck bed. As he walked back toward Ambrose, Bonnie Rowe got out and ran up to him. She wrapped her arms around him tightly, saying, again, "Thank you, thank you," until he pried her arms loose. Ambrose's dad's face betrayed true disbelief when he came back to the truck.

"What happened?" Ambrose asked.

"He was already passed out. Instantly. Imagine that."

"What'd she want?"

"Somebody to stick up for her, I guess." And they drove away, but Ambrose watched his dad's eyes remain on the rearview. "That man's gonna kill somebody."

6

Lily came home to her place on Waquaheag, mentally preparing already for what she anticipated would be some kind of showdown with her boss. She carried her dinner, a plastic container of cold pasta salad from the good deli in Nevin. The clouds had blown in over the moon. Rain was coming, and she could smell it in the air, cold and clean and faintly metallic. She paused in front of her house, almost pleased with it. She hadn't had to do much to get it in the end.

When she was almost nineteen, after she and Seb had scattered her mother's ashes in the side yard, she simply asked him if she should talk to a lawyer about what they owed and what to do about it, and he said he'd sign the place over. He didn't want to carry the cost or think about it anymore. He said he was heartbroken for them both, and it was the only right thing to do. He didn't know that she'd talked already to a Hartford lawyer a few times over the years. She was going to get that house, one way or another, and it was good for everyone that the old man didn't try to put up a fight. She'd been paying rent on it since she was fourteen, when she got a part-time job at the general store making sandwiches, breaking down boxes to start. By then, no one had seen her dad or brother in town for a year. Seb tore up most of the rent checks she sent. Either way, she mailed them every month, certified, though they were neighbors and it would've been easier for her just to leave them in his mailbox.

Stepping up onto the front porch, she ran her hand over the cracked wooden rail. She'd painted it black but had never fixed it. That was just about the only repair she hadn't made to the house. She'd renovated the kitchen and bathrooms. Redone the roof, paved the driveway, hydro-seeded the lawn. Finished the basement, the attic. She'd demolished the old shed, where her dad used to take her brother, and she'd done her best to erase its mark on the yard. But she hadn't fixed that rail.

And every morning, every night, she touched it, and she thought about her brother and his sacrifice. She thought about when she was twelve, but had felt much older than that, as she watched Ray shoot his two hunting arrows, over and over, into the back of a soggy, broken-down couch in the side yard. The couch had been Bob Bainer's, but it'd been chewed up and pissed on by mice and filled with the seeds they'd stashed for winter. Ray had dragged it out of the house and across the snow crust. He'd used a can of orange spray paint to put a target on it, which was a circle with a squiggly stick figure body, arms, and legs. His bull's-eye was a human head.

The bow was a gift from a neighbor of theirs in Erie, New York, where they'd been for a year before Macoun. The neighbor, a man named Figlio, had noticed that Ray slept some nights in his father's truck. Their place then had only one bedroom, and Lily got the living room futon, though they shared it on the coldest nights. When Abe Rowe had gone off again, so long it seemed he might never come back this time, Mr. Figlio invited Ray to stay in his guest room while his wife was visiting family in Toronto. Ray was fourteen, but they drank some Molson beers together and Figlio showed the boy his collection of guns. They made plans to go deer hunting when the season came. Ray got the bow and arrows so he could practice until then. He stayed over at Figlio's in the guest room for two nights.

On the second night, though, Abe returned late. Lily woke to him shaking her, demanding to know where Ray was. His breath was hot and rank. She was confused. In the dark, she didn't need to see him to know his eyes would be as impenetrable as a brick wall. He shook her harder and she told him. She said Ray had been given permission to use the Figlios' guest room, and she felt immediately guilty. She'd been so startled and afraid that it seemed she'd betrayed her brother. Her father stormed out of the house. It was well before dawn when he started pounding on the neighbor's door. Lily came out into the front yard, barefoot in a foot of snow, saying, "Daddy, please."

The houses were close together and some of the neighbors had called the cops on them before. But Abe didn't relent. She could see the steam of his breath in the porch light.

"You think I don't know what you're doing with my son?" he said. She couldn't hear what Figlio was saying, but she'd seen this act before. Her dad had a knack for identifying a predator type, and he had asked men like this to watch Ray a few times, and once to watch her. Then he'd come to the so-called rescue, demanding money and threatening to call the cops. Lily knew he'd never call them, but that was his bluff, his con. Dangle his kids like bait. It'd worked more often than it hadn't. Still, it was hard to ever predict what her father might do, outside of knowing that it wouldn't be good.

She saw him relent at Mr. Figlio's door, and a minute later, she watched an envelope come through the mail slot. Her dad pulled a stack of money from it, and she could see him smiling. It proved to be his biggest score yet. Then she saw Ray slip out the back door with his new bow and arrows wrapped in a towel and a plastic shopping bag swinging behind him. The money diverted her father enough to prevent any further violence. He was in a chipper mood that morning, shuffling around the house, whistling the theme song to *The Andy Griffith Show.* Lily had never seen the show, only knew that melody as his happy song. And flush with cash, the Rowes were on the move again that afternoon.

The kids were put in the bed of the truck wearing all the clothes they had, their paltry possessions piled in around them. Over them, Abe had roped down the tarp, in which he'd stabbed an air slit with his combat knife. This was how they'd traveled between temporary homes in Pennsylvania, Ohio, Indiana, Missouri, all the way back west.

"If the cops pull us over," he told the kids, "you keep your goddamn traps shut. If they find you, they'll put you in places where you'd rather be dead. Trust me." Abe had been a ward of the state as a boy, Lily knew. The things he did, to Ray especially, he said were nothing compared to what'd been done to him. That's how he justified it, she supposed. That's the only reality he'd ever known, and so to him, that's how the world was, and how it would always be, for them anyway. It was pointless to try to change that.

"I'm sorry," Lily told Ray as the tarp flapped against their faces in the highway wind.

Ray shifted on top of his new hunting bow, which he'd kept hidden. He yelled so Lily could hear him, "Once you're big enough or he's gone once and for all, I swear, I'm going to Alaska to hunt and live off the land and kiss all these bullshit people goodbye."

"What happened with Mister Figlio?" she shouted back.

"Nothing," he said, before filling her in about the beer and the guns. "He was working up to something, I think, but I would've kicked that little bitch in the balls. It was just too cold in the truck. He gave me beer, though. And we had pizza."

"Pizza?" Her stomach ached. Her teeth chattered in the cold. "What kind?"

"Only cheese," he said. "One of those make-at-home ones."

"Was it good?"

"I saved you some." From the plastic shopping bag beside him, he pulled out a stiff cold square of pizza with only a couple of bites taken from it. "Here." He propped the tarp higher above them with one hand and gave it over. She devoured it, muttering, with her mouth full, that it was the best she'd ever had.

"Don't save any," Ray said. "He might find it." Then he unwrapped one of the arrows from the towel under him and held the pointed head of it close to his face. He stared at it, spinning it slowly in his hand, for miles and miles. She didn't have to ask what he was thinking about. They played a game sometimes where they fantasized about how they'd do it. To Lily, it was just talk.

7

Cale started surfing at a time when he didn't care if he lived or died. He was in his early thirties when he arrived in Hawaii, with almost nothing beyond the idea of suicide. He survived those first nights with working girls whisked away from a Waikiki side street constellated with neon signs. These women, speakers of little English always, he overpaid to indulge a request they often found strange. To hold him while he wept and never tell. Though he now had a reputation to protect and didn't need that anymore, he knew in some way they'd saved him.

One morning shortly after his arrival, he was drunk, sitting alone on the beach at Ala Moana, feeling hollowed out and thinking little. A shirtless man in his seventies walked by. He had long white hair, but he was spry and fit, hauling two surfboards, one under each arm. He gestured to a board and said, "Hey, you wanna try ride?"

Cale shrugged, said fuck it, and paddled out, flopping and flailing. He got tossed off the board before he made it through the reef. In the churning wash of whitewater, he hit his forehead on a rock. He came to the surface as the next wave broke on top of him. The older guy, whose name he learned was Kawika Arnold, came back and helped him get to shore. As Cale caught his breath on the beach, blood ran down his face and dripped off his chin, clotting the sand. But the next day, he felt like trying it again, and then the next day too.

A decade later, as he stood on that same beach, strapping the Velcro cuff of his board leash to his left ankle, he thought about Kawika's random act of generosity toward a stranger. That moment had changed his life, it turned out. Surfing had given him something to do instead of drinking, and a reason to go to bed early and rise before dawn, when the waves were usually best. In the water, he'd met the CEO of Ono Real Estate, Glen Igashi, who gave him his first job in that industry, and in time, to his surprise, he'd been able to make something of himself. Not as he was, but as Reese. He found the surf cleared his mind, which is why he thought it might help him forget some of the guilt and heartache he felt after breaking up with Janelle, which days later still hurt.

Cale slid onto his board and glided out. The cool water tightened his chest. He paddled out to deeper water, but stopped. He sat up and stared at the horizon. The shades of blue, sea and sky, blended into one, with no clear separation. He found himself suddenly adrift, confused, wondering if he was even there. His mind was playing an old warped trick on him, he knew, but he didn't know why. It'd been years since he'd been troubled by his memories, but he assumed it was because of Janelle that he felt as if he were grieving again, going along fine and then suddenly upside down, seeing a flash of an old image in his mind that contained too much to bear. He found himself thinking about Lily again, remembering the first time they ever spoke.

It was during Thanksgiving break, November 1992, when Cale was still in the eighth grade and Lily was in the seventh, same as Ambrose. Cale went to see the tree his grandmother had carved, marking the floodwater. It was something he'd been meaning to do since he'd learned of the connection, but he'd been busy with school and his junior high soccer team, on which he was the captain and leading scorer. Ambrose was a defensive star on the same team. A bruiser who was not afraid to go up against anyone. Already there was talk of Macoun finally having a shot at a state championship, in the small-town class anyway, when the Casey boys went up to varsity.

The season had been over for weeks by the time Cale set out in his down-filled parka, wool knit hat, and gloves. His dog, Sammy, bounding off ahead. They lived in the same house his father had as a boy, so he crossed the same field his grandmother had the day she disappeared, and he took the same path into those woods. A narrow trail went through a sunken scattered stone wall and a thicket of prickers and sumac before widening into what had been used as a wagon road a hundred years before. It led down into a small valley, where Flash Brook snaked through the bottom. Cale's dad was a carpenter, a homebuilder, held in the utmost regard. He'd constructed a good bridge over the brook before the boys were born. It was much longer and taller than required, designed to withstand a hundred-year flood. The yellow of the pressure-treated wood had faded some, but the structure remained as sound as ever. Going over it, Cale wondered how his grandmother had gotten over that brook, swollen as it surely had been, to get to the larger and more powerful Fox. He knew his father had built a similarly extensive bridge across that brook too, and Cale imagined them both for the first time as tributes to her, or meditations.

A trail started on the opposite bank, and he followed it up the other side of the valley through a stand of black birch. He tore a twig from one of the saplings and took in the scent. He and Ambrose had tried once to make their own birch beer from it, boiling skinned limbs with water and sugar. The end product tasted like sweet, watery dirt, which marked the end of that experiment and gave them a greater appreciation for the bottled Avery's at the general store.

Cale crested a hill, careful of his footing. He tried to keep his crunching steps as quiet as possible, with the hope of coming upon turkey, deer, even a coyote. His father had taught him how to walk in the woods, how to pay attention in what he called an alertness in trance. He came to an overlook above Fox Brook, not far from the tree he was after. But rather than wildlife, what he saw was a person sitting on a flat rock fifty feet down the slope. It was a girl in a hooded sweatshirt, no coat. Her back was to him. It was almost as startling as coming upon a bear, because he'd never encountered anyone else in those woods, even if he'd sometimes found the bits of trash they'd left behind. She was leaning against a white birch, the type some call the watchful tree because the black markings on its pale bark look like eyes. She stood suddenly and turned, tensed and ready to run. He knew that it was Lily and that she lived in that rundown house up on Waquaheag Road, a half mile east. She held a book to her chest. She relaxed slightly when she saw him, but still appeared ready to make a break for it.

"Hi," he said.

"Hi," she said, her voice soft but confident. It was the first time he'd ever heard her speak.

"Didn't mean to spook you."

"You didn't."

"I'm Cale."

"I know."

"We're on the same bus."

"I know."

"In the mornings anyway." He scratched the side of his head underneath his hat. "I took the late bus after school in the fall. Soccer."

"Good for you."

"My mom picks us up now after sometimes." He grimaced at the sound of his pointless chatter. He heard movement behind him and the tinkling of Sammy's collar and was relieved when the dog came bounding in behind him.

"Stay," he commanded, but Sammy ran right past him, wagging her tail, her whole body wriggling as she got to Lily. "She's friendly," he told her, and then to the dog, "Leave her alone. Come back here, Sammy. Come."

The dog didn't listen, but Lily rustled her ears, clearly happier interacting with the dog than with Cale. It eased the awkwardness, and he walked down toward her to get Sammy, who took off running along the brook bank, sniffing after a trail of rabbit tracks.

"Sorry. She's still kind of a puppy."

"Because she doesn't listen to you?"

He shrugged and looked away, feeling the heat rise in his face. "She sometimes does."

"My old neighbor had a dog like that once."

"Where was that?"

"I don't know." She crouched down to the rock. "A few places ago."

"What're you doing out here?"

"Reading."

"You're freezing."

"I'm fine."

"You just have a sweatshirt on?"

"I said I'm fine." She stood again.

"Okay," he said. "Just, why would you read out here in the cold?"

"Why don't you fuck off?"

Cale's mouth opened, but he said nothing. Every morning on the school bus, he'd seen her sitting in the front seat behind the driver, curled against the window, silent. He'd often stared at her, but he could never catch her eye. In the hallways at school, she moved fast, head down. But there was something that had fascinated him about her since he first saw her at the general store, buying bread and cold cuts and milk with pocket change even though there were racks of candy and chips all around her.

In the glimpses of her most mornings, it had become harder and harder for him to try to ignore her. Even with the stories he'd heard from other kids about her father's firing at the dump swap shack for jacking off on the job, or the ones about her mother, Bonnie, moping blankly through the IGA grocery, and then acting wild at the Fish House bar, arm around a plumber, arm around a roofer, when her own husband had gone off again on a drunk somewhere. Worst of all, there was her brother, Ray, who rode the school bus with them. He sat in the last seat, with empty rows in front of him, on the days he went to school, and kids piled three into a seat to avoid being too close. Normally, he was quiet, though sometimes he screamed. Usually, he was calm, until he went berserk and began pounding the back of the seat in front of him. Often, he smoked cigarettes, and the bus driver said nothing.

In spite of these things, Cale thought more about Lily than he should have. Some guys on his soccer team, friends, joked about her, and he would chuckle along half-heartedly. There was seemingly nothing special about her, and yet he felt she truly was special. It was something he couldn't explain. He just felt it.

"Sorry," he told her again.

"My dad's home," she said. "He was gone for a while, and now he's back. So that's why I'd rather be out here, okay?"

Cale took off his hat. "You want this?"

"No."

"It's cold." He hung the hat on a hemlock branch. "I'll leave it here in case you change your mind."

"You got a million of them, huh?"

"What?"

"You can keep your little hat."

He turned away, leaving it. "I should go find my dog."

"What's with your family, huh?" she said. "You think you're saints or something? You think you're saviors?"

"My family?"

"I've known plenty of people like you. You think you're the good guys, but you're not. What you give isn't a gift at all, in the end. It's all more trouble than it's worth."

He looked at her, stunned once more. "I don't think you know me at all."

"I do," she said. "And you tell your dad to stay away from us. If he's trying to mess around with my mom, my dad'll kill him. He was in Vietnam."

"So was mine," Cale said.

"I'm just trying to help you," she said. "My dad's gone crazy on people before, and now he's back. He doesn't want anyone's pity or people snooping around. You tell your dad to stay away, if he knows what's good for him. It's like that with us."

Cale walked off, dazed. He was back in the field by his house by the time he remembered the dog, who ran up behind him, and the tree he'd gone to see but never did.

8

Ambrose didn't believe what his brother told him about Bonnie Rowe. They were shooting hoops in the driveway, playing HORSE. It was the last day of their winter school break. They were on the junior high basketball team together, where Ambrose was outscoring his older brother. Now, he was winning the first game of HORSE too. He had no letters, but Cale had three. Neither wore a jacket or gloves and their hands were red and stiff from the cold.

"That puts you at HOR," Ambrose said.

"Whore? Watch your mouth, you nasty little pooch," Cale said. Inane insults were part of how they competed. Cale took a shot that clanked off the rim. "I did that on purpose."

"I continue to have no letters, while you remain a prostitute. But I'm about to make you an HORS d'oeuvre." Ambrose took the ball behind a yew. "Show me that cocktail weenie." He heaved up the shot and missed the backboard entirely.

Cale went to get the ball. "Being a whore wouldn't be so bad, would it? Everybody kind of is in a way, right?"

"Think about all the gremlins you'd have to bang," Ambrose said.

"Like who?" Cale asked, scratching a few pimples along his jawline.

"How about Missus Lionel, the lunch lady?"

"She's not so bad."

"How much?" Ambrose said.

"I'd do it for, I don't know, four hundred bucks?"

Ambrose laughed. "Puke."

"I need a new mountain bike." Cale hucked up a shot from behind the hoop that bounced off the rim. "That was very close."

"Not really." Ambrose got to the bouncing ball and dribbled it. "Here comes Hakeem Olajuwon, baby," he said, doing his best to conjure the NBA star.

"How about Polly McDonald?" Cale asked, about their neighbor, a kind octogenarian who collected unwashed yogurt containers in her sink. She hired the boys once in a while to do chores, but the smell in her house of rotten yogurt was so strong that they'd asked their mother to say they could only do outdoor jobs.

"I think we have different career ambitions." Ambrose sunk a shot from the free throw line, which was a crack in the driveway.

"One more," Cale said, getting the ball. "And actually think about this one."

"Who?"

Cale took the ball to the free throw line. "Bonnie Rowe." He hit the shot.

Ambrose shook his head. "It's ridiculous that you're not a shrimp cocktail yet. But you're just delaying the inevitable."

"What do you think of her?"

"Who cares?"

"Just answer it."

"She's a freak, dude, as far as I know. So what?" Ambrose bent his knees, preparing to take another shot from the free throw line. "I'm just going to bleed you out this way. You won't hit another gimme."

Cale stepped in front of him. "You're not even thinking about it."

"About what?" Ambrose stood up, holding the ball at his hip.

Cale took a step closer. "It's the game."

"The game is HORSE. Now, get out of my face."

"It's the game within the game."

"That's me talking shit to get in your head."

"It's the game within the game's game, then," Cale said.

"I don't know what you're talking about, but back up."

"Or what?"

"Or I'll whoop your worrywart ass."

"You think you're so tough."

"I don't think it."

"You're an idiot."

Ambrose whipped the basketball at him. Cale blocked it with his forearms and it bounced off into the frozen mulch bed behind the hoop. He ran at Ambrose, who stepped aside and grabbed him by the head and flung him onto the hard lawn.

"You and these Rowes," Ambrose said.

"What are you talking about?"

"I see you looking at Lily on the bus, dude. And now you're getting worked up talking about her mom?"

Cale stood up and faced Ambrose like he might take a swing at him.

"I wouldn't do it if I were you, Cale."

A car pulled into the driveway then, Joan Gindewin's blue Jeep. She tapped the horn twice in greeting. The boys waved. Their mother came out the front door, wearing her canvas barn coat and a white knit hat. She said, "What's going on here, boys?"

"Nothing, Mom," Ambrose said.

"No fighting," she said.

Neither responded.

"Promise me. No fighting. Promise?"

"Okay," Cale said.

"Promise," she said.

"Promise," he said.

Ambrose watched her walk toward Joan's car. "Missus Gindewin and I need to go help with something." Their mother, a pediatric nurse and devout Catholic, often volunteered at their church in the next town over. "Your dad will be home soon." She got into the Jeep, which backed out of the driveway.

"You want to hear something weird?" Cale said.

"Everything you say is weird."

Cale looked at him.

Ambrose tensed up. "What?"

"It's probably not true," Cale said, but then he told Ambrose what Lily had suggested about their dad and Bonnie Rowe. He told him about Lily's warning that her father would kill theirs if he kept coming around.

"No way," Ambrose said.

"Yeah." Cale went and picked up the basketball. "Who's shot is it anyway?"

"I don't want to play anymore." Ambrose went inside and up to his room. He hit play on his boom box. He listened to Nirvana's first tape, *Bleach*, which he'd gotten after wearing out their second tape in his Walkman. He sat on his bed, thinking about that day in the Fish House parking lot when Abe Rowe had stared at him and insulted them, and then his drunk wife was hanging all over his dad. He wondered then if maybe his dad and Bonnie Rowe had known each other already.

That night, when his father came in to say goodnight, Ambrose wanted to ask him about Bonnie Rowe, but to his surprise, he heard himself ask, "Did you ever kill anyone in the war?"

"I was mostly on boats," he answered.

"How come you never talk about that?" Ambrose asked.

"I don't not talk about it."

Cale came into the room, looking for a book.

"So, tell me, then." Ambrose shifted under the covers. "You never tell me anything."

"I tell you both I love you, don't I?"

"Ew," Ambrose said.

His father nodded, thought for a moment, and then took a seat in the spindle-backed chair beside the bed.

He said, "In the Pacific, east of Hawaii, you can smell the flowers days before you see land." At least that's how it'd been, he went on, that afternoon in the winter of 1969, when he was nineteen and bound first for Pearl Harbor aboard the USS *Tortuga*. It was a floral wind that welcomed him to war. Different from any other he'd known, including the best of his memory, like wood smoke blowing in clear fall air, or summer breezes draped in cut grass and charcoal barbecue. The wet gusts of spring that burst open with birdsong, and a strange warm wind he felt once at the end of a different winter that carried with it the hint of a neighbor's maple syrup on the boil. He was around the boys' age then, and out chopping wood beside the house while his father napped in a chair inside. That maple syrup wind came in and cut through the cold metal smell of the maul and the scent of his leather gloves sweated through at the wrist creases. He breathed it all in, with the wooden handle in his hands and the head of the maul still ringing from good use. And what welled up in him then was gratitude in its silent symphony.

He remembered this wind, he said, this singular wind of home, as the distant flowers and fruits of Hawaii sweetened the thick, salted air. Breathing it in, he watched the dull gray blade of the ship hull carve through the water and unfurl it in broadening ribbons of cream. He still couldn't see land, just the endless blue. And with every unseen turn of the propellers, he traveled farther into it. Farther away from home, forever, he felt. It was a one-way journey, like most for the living, and he could not know if he'd ever return. His winds, his woodpiles, dissipated in the distant dark.

"You didn't answer the question," Ambrose said.

"No?"

"I asked if you ever killed anyone. Or did anyone ever try to kill you?"

"It was war," he said. "But I told you, I was mostly on boats."

9

Leaving her house at dawn, Lily ran her hand down the cracked porch railing she'd never repaired. There were some things, she knew, that could not be fixed, could not be forgotten. She looked out across the yard, where she'd watched Ray stomp back and forth in his black combat boots, shooting his arrows into his couch target and then pulling them out again.

The day the rail cracked, she knew, was in mid-January 1993. Sunny and windless, but a few degrees below freezing. Despite the cold, Ray wore his black sleeveless t-shirt and torn jeans. He was short and seemingly full grown, though wiry and strong. His dark hair was longish and jagged. He'd cut it himself. The whiskers had come in on his mustache and a little bit on his chin. Lily sat on the steps, in a jacket that was too thin and socks that had holes for heels, watching him shoot. His aim was getting to be pretty good, and they both hoped he'd be able to get a deer someday soon, even a rabbit, or a squirrel.

On the edge of the yard, she saw one of Seb Bainer's barn cats, a young tabby, picking its way through the underbrush. Seb lived on the other side of the hayfield next door in a cabin at the end of a long dirt driveway. Lily often went down to his barn to see the cats. There were five, though Seb didn't know whether it was four or six. Coyotes got some, new ones appeared. He filled big bowls of food and water every morning so the cats would hang around to keep the mice and chipmunks down. They weren't pets to him. They were part of the farm and served a purpose, had a job. Seb had only bothered to name a couple, but Lily had her own names for them all. The one she saw in her yard then she'd already named Jack, for "Jack-o'-Lantern." She went inside to get her boots on to go see the cat. When she came back out, she saw Ray taking aim at Jack with his bow.

"Ray, no!" she shouted.

The cat spooked and Ray's arrow sailed over it, clinking off a pine trunk.

"God dammit, Lily."

"That's Mister Bainer's cat."

"What do you care?"

"That's Jack."

"I need to be able to hit anything."

"Why?"

"You want Daddy around forever?" Ray huffed off into the woods to fetch the arrow. From the pocket of her hooded sweatshirt, Lily took the winter hat Cale had left on the hemlock branch. It read *Casey Homes*, and it still smelled like him, his shampoo, a type she couldn't place. From it, too, she got the feeling of a cozy house with a good fire and things baking. Bread, chicken, an abundance. Safety and warmth. Peace. A picture of happiness.

She'd thought about Cale before but had quickly shut down any dreaming. He was a soccer star, well-liked by many, an A student, she knew. And she was a Rowe. Though her grades had steadily risen since their arrival in Macoun, she was still doing homework most nights hungry and worried and, this time of year, cold. At home, an unsettling disturbance was more common than a working light. Plus, they'd moved around so much, she was always starting and stopping on some subject or other, coming into the curriculum at different points, at schools with different priorities.

She went looking for Jack the cat, calling to him softly. She stopped when she saw a white pickup truck pull up in front of the house and park. Her instinct was to hide, and she slid behind one of the pines. She heard the truck door open and shut. Carefully, she leaned around the tree and saw Cale's dad, Mr. Casey, approach their house, carrying in one arm a brown paper grocery bag. He knocked on the front door. Her mother was inside sleeping, but Lily knew she wouldn't hear him, or get up if she did, not today.

Today was one of her down days, when she barely moved. Mr. Casey looked around, put the bag on the warped and peeling front porch, and went back to his truck. That was the fourth time he'd shown up unannounced with groceries. The third time he'd done that, her father had been the one to find the food. He went berserk and kicked Ray twice in the ribs for talking too much at school, saying they "didn't need no charity," before taking all the food for himself.

Lily waited for the truck to go back down Waquaheag the way it'd come, and then she hurried to the front porch. She called for Ray but got no response. Inside the bag there was bread and milk and butter and cheese and turkey and soup and oranges. The oranges filled her with a swell of excitement and she bit into the bitter skin of one to expedite the peeling and sucked some of the juice from the fruit before she could tear the skin off. She felt an energy surge through her body, and she closed her eyes, taken away for an instant. She ate that orange, consciously slowing her pace to make it last. She was opening the seal on the bag of cheese when she heard the sound of tires in the driveway behind her. She flinched, preparing to run, but stopped herself. Some predators, she'd learned in a book, only chase you if you run. She straightened up and turned to face her father, caught.

He flicked a cigarette butt out the half-open window, which was stuck permanently that way. "Where'd you get that hat?"

She'd forgotten she was wearing it. She held up the cheese. "Who keeps leaving this crap?"

"What's it say on there?" He got out of the truck, unfolding his stiff long legs. He walked over, a towering figure, stooped. He looked her up and down, assessing her coolly. He ripped the cheese from her hand and flipped it into the yard.

She lowered her head but stood her ground. If you encounter a black bear in the forest, you don't run. You want to look big. She had a hard time looking big. And with him, she thought, that could be perceived as a challenge, a threat.

"Who gave you all this?" he said.

"No one. I don't know."

"Sounds like you got a boyfriend. That asshole Casey. That old man. He's your boyfriend, is he?"

"No, sir."

"So, you're grown enough for that now, eh, girl?"

"No, sir."

"Why don't we see about that, huh?" He was blackout drunk, she could tell. That's when he did things he didn't remember, so no apologies were necessary. When he got like this, she'd learned, you couldn't stop him. It was like a river coming down on you, and you had to try to divert him slightly some other way. You couldn't dam him. If you tried, you drowned.

"We got some bread and eggs," she said, her voice and eyes low. "You want me to make you an egg sandwich with butter and cheese?"

"I ate," he said.

"Really? What'd you have?"

"Shut up." He spit. "I want you to come with me. I want to show you something in the shed."

"Mom asked me to wake her when you got home."

"You come with me now."

"Mom asked me to wake her." She felt a swell of panic.

"It'll only take a minute," he said. "You'll like it, now that you're grown. I promise."

Her legs felt ready to give out. She could run, but if he caught her, she didn't know. If she got away, she'd have to stay out for a night, maybe two, until he forgot again. But she'd noticed the way he'd started looking at her. She'd begun to doubt that he'd keep forgetting.

Ray came out of the woods and into the yard, no bow or arrows, moving toward them. He said, "What's going on, Daddy?"

"Your sister's all grown, with boyfriends coming over. She wants to see the shed."

"I'll go with you, Daddy." He stepped in front of her, saying quietly, "There's spiders in there. She's too little. She's afraid of spiders."

Abe stared at his son. The skin around his eyes crinkled and he tilted his head slightly. "What a goddamn shame," he said. "I've raised a little cocksucker." With an explosive fury, he grabbed Ray by the shoulders and chucked him toward the front porch. The back of his head hit the railing. Lily screamed at the sound of the cracking, unsure if it was the wood or her brother's skull. On his side, Ray writhed and rocked on the hard snow-covered ground, eyes shut, mouth open, silent. Lily rushed to him. Her father kicked the bag of groceries off the step. An orange rolled past the children as he creaked onto the porch, his boots dragging and knocking.

A few weeks later, Lily's father tried to take her to the shed again, and this time she did run. She hid shivering up in the hayloft at Seb Bainer's for a weekend, using an oil-stained drop cloth as a blanket. When she came home, tentatively, creeping around the house at first, to see what was what, she learned that Ray had actually done it. He'd killed their father, smashed his head in with a cinder block, and then he'd waited for her to come help him clean up the mess.

10

C. Reese Casey had a good chuckle. His assistant, Derek, had proposed some social media posts to help sell a twelve-million-dollar mansion, but the only fact he'd chosen to feature was that the property was "conveniently located" near a shopping mall. Reese called him into his office, which was bright with sunlight streaming through the floor-to-ceiling windows.

Derek, tall and lanky, entered and smiled, revealing his braces. He had thick hair cut straight across the front, three inches above his eyebrows. His medical mask was pulled down over his chin. They were two of only a handful of people who'd started coming back into the office, not that Derek had a choice.

Reese held up the printed paper. "What the hell is this?"

"A paper?"

"More specific."

"A white piece of paper."

"It's your social."

"Do you like it?"

"When someone asks you 'What the hell is this?' do they usually like it?"

"I didn't hear that part."

"That's the first thing I said to you."

"I was just so excited." He looked down at the floor. "You never let me write social, Reese."

He sighed. "Don't call me that."

"Sorry, Mister Casey."

"Not that either."

"Okay. Sir?"

"Whatever. Just, take another run at it, if you want, okay? But try to put yourself in the potential buyer's shoes. If you want to go into this business ultimately, that's something to keep in mind. This won't be a local person, unfortunately. It'll be some software billionaire or some oligarch peddler of liquefied dino bones, you know? A second- or third-home owner who wants to brag about having their own little piece of private pineapple. So think about that exclusivity, paradise, rather than the nearby shopping malls, you follow? Imagine people worse than me, shitty haoles, the ones who are ruining this place for us all. That's our buyer. Sorry."

"Got it." Derek nodded with confidence.

"Do you? Because I don't even know what I'm saying right now." He was tired. The night before, he couldn't fall back asleep after a nightmare had woken him. In it, he was slogging through the muck of a black swamp. Roots wrapped around his ankles, pulling him down. He looked between his legs as he sank into the mud and saw something in the dark water that seemed to pack his lungs with snow. He felt as if there were a distant hellhound tearing across the water, coming. Coming. But what he'd seen had been an innocuous thing. In the center of that chaotic darkness. In the dream swamp. A pale stick, about an arm's length, of birch.

He didn't understand what it meant exactly, but it filled him with an old familiar fear. All day he'd felt oddly fragile. It reminded him of times in the past when he might be overcome inexplicably by a three-second sobbing jag, precipitated by the sight of a circling hawk or a plate of pancakes.

"Maybe you're just still upset," Derek said.

"About what?"

"Your girlfriend." He glanced at him. "Your ex, anyway?"

"Who told you about that?" Cale rubbed his forehead and sighed.

"I can just tell," he said.

"Hm."

"You seemed much happier with her."

"Okay, that'll be it for now."

"Sorry. Just, I get it, you know? And you're not alone, okay?"

Cale stared at him. "Yes, I am."

"No, a lot of men have intimacy issues." Derek's cheeks reddened. "I know I do."

Cale almost laughed, until he noticed how painful that statement appeared to be for the goofy young man. He felt sorry for him, but then it occurred to him that maybe Derek was right, and he felt worse about himself. He knew that sooner or later Janelle would've seen through the glossy exterior nacred around his self-loathing, and what she would've seen instead was a horror. But by then he would've wasted too much of her time. He understood he was a phony, full of shit, and he felt suddenly sick about it.

"Well, thanks for sharing," he said.

"Yes, um. Yes." Derek nodded and walked backward out of the office. He shut the door.

Cale spun in his chair. He looked out the window at the fronds of the palm trees wagging in the breeze along a fairway. He considered the idea of intimacy issues, and it seemed like something you'd see on the covers of magazines in line at the grocery store. Which celeb was banging what, intimacy issues, and recipes for low-carb cakes. No, his situation, his life, went well beyond something as simple as that, he felt. Still, he wondered if maybe there were secrets he could share with Janelle, like she'd wanted. He missed her, and he realized he'd lost her, and others too, friends and lovers, preemptively. It seemed better that they thought he was just a regular asshole than that they knew the truth about how awful he was. And who could he trust, really, in the end? He had so much to lose now: money, status, career, good food and wine and sex and surf. His house, his car, just the possibilities, Paris in the spring. But even when he had nothing, that was much preferred, he thought, to a life in a cell, even if he'd been living in his own kind of prison most of his life. It'd taken a long time to get out of it.

He thought about what he could tell Janelle, what would be enough. Maybe he could reveal what had happened with Bonnie Rowe, how it had confused him as a fourteen-year-old kid, and after, without getting too close to the things he couldn't say.

He started thinking back to what happened, years before, when he was preparing for his confirmation in the church, the final phase of Sunday school, at the insistence of his mother. They'd gone to church most weeks when he was a kid, and he'd been afraid of death and the endless suffering of hell for as long as he could remember. For him, Sunday mornings had been about boredom and fear, endurance. Strange smells, strange priest, a lot of singing off-key.

And yet, it was the prospect of a sin, his father's sin, that'd upset him so much after that first reverberating exchange in the woods with Lily Rowe. The thought of his dad and Mrs. Rowe was hard to fathom. For one thing, his mother was a good woman, a great woman. And most people in town said Mrs. Rowe was a loon, which seemed unfair and overly simple, dumb, to Cale even then. But the reported sightings of her around that little town were often so odd and over-the-top, it was hard to know what to make of her. Seemingly vacant, and then several times, he'd heard through friends who'd heard through siblings and uncles, she was nearly swinging from the wicker chandelier down at the Fish House bar, showing flashes of a strange beauty and a wildness that'd threatened to lure a few local men away from their wives for a night. In a place where almost nothing unusual seemed to happen, Bonnie Rowe proved to be worth talking about. The wheel spinners of the local rumor mill picked up their Porta Phones and cranked the dials on their rotaries.

It was possible, Cale thought, that Bonnie had suffered under the wrath of a wicked man, who'd likely suffered himself. That was one fact of religion he'd held on to, the universal suffering, albeit in different shades. But at fourteen, he didn't care so much why a dangerous stranger might've been the way she was. He was just worried that his father would tear their family apart, and his response to this fear was to separate himself from his dad. To treat him coldly, as if Lily's suggestion were, in fact, gospel. She set that earwig of adultery burrowing into his brain as he trained to become a confirmed soldier of Christ.

Cale's teacher at St. Francis Church encouraged all the kids in the confirmation class to go out into the community and do good works. That was part of fulfilling their spiritual journey, fighting for good over evil. It gave Cale the idea to go see Mrs. Rowe himself. That seemed simpler and less consequential than asking his father directly if he was having an affair. Perhaps more importantly, it gave him an opportunity to get closer to Lily, to see how she really lived.

So, on the first day of the February school break, he went out into the cold woods again to make the trek to Waquaheag Road. Six inches of snow had fallen the night before, but it was light and dry, well below the tops of his boots. It was the kind of fresh quiet in the woods that usually put him at ease. But the trembling in his stomach increased as he crossed the bridge over Fox Brook and left his family's property. The owner of the next plot of land was a man named Seymour, a reclusive mechanic with forty acres and at least four tree stands. Cale's mother always asked that he and Ambrose wear bright orange hats when they went out into the woods, so Seymour or some other hunter didn't accidentally shoot them. But Cale was dressed for camouflage, as he moved on, leaving clear tracks in the snow behind him. He broke his own way through the brush and laurel. His mouth became so dry it was a chore to swallow. Eventually, through a stand of leafless swamp maples, he could see the faded red paint of Seb Bainer's barn. Behind it, he moved north along a ridge toward the Rowes'.

His plan that day was merely to do some reconnaissance. The next phase, for tomorrow or the day after, was to tell Bonnie that he was helping neighbors with yard work, for his church. The connection was pretty thin, he knew, but he wanted to look her in the eye and see if she betrayed any indication that might confirm what Lily had said. For months, the prospect of his dad and her mom had nagged at him to varying degrees. It had no good clean outcome that he could imagine. His best scenario, he knew, would be that Lily was a liar, and then he could forget about her. But he didn't feel that he'd stop thinking about her and he didn't want to. She'd begun intruding upon his mind more and more. In his bed alone, he imagined them walking out of the prom together. In church, staring at the hymnal, he wondered what she looked like naked. He had fantasies of another chance meeting in the woods, which would lead to them skinny-dipping in the cold brook and rolling on the mossy bank beneath the brightest stars.

Approaching the Rowes' house, these visions of Lily collided with a range of fears, Ray chief among them, even though Ray hadn't had an outburst on the school bus in several weeks. The heightened tension that had seemed to turn the bus into a pressure chamber had lessened. Before, Ray would scream out of nowhere and no one would turn around to look, at first because of fear, and later because of boredom. But something seemed to have changed in him. A calmness softened the atmosphere, and Cale wondered if Ray had become medicated, properly tranquilized. Still, Cale remained alert as he crept up toward the Rowes' house. He went as far as a big pine a few dozen feet from their yard. It was behind a ramshackle shed of gray boards. From there, he could see the back of the battered house and the beat-up tan Datsun pickup in the driveway. He could witness the comings and goings as he developed his plan. He studied the back door, a torn screen still in it. When he did come to speak to Bonnie, he thought, he'd go to that door. He could look into the house before he knocked and not be seen from the road.

The cold wind blew through the trees around him. He heard the scratching and clucking of a squirrel overhead and farther off the shriek of a red-tailed hawk. He crouched by the pine, watching, spying, thinking. The cold started to set into him after half an hour. His only useful observations were the way there, the big pine, and the back door. He was thinking he'd give it just a few more minutes before he left, when the shed door creaked open. He stiffened, though he assumed it was the work of the wind. Then Ray came out wearing an olive military jacket that was so big on him it looked like a robe. He unzipped his fly and took a leak right there in the yard a few steps from the shed. Cale's breath caught in his throat and he pulled back behind the trunk. He listened, his pulse thumping. He heard Ray clear his throat and spit, moving away. Cale peered around the tree and watched him get in the truck in the driveway. It'd been backed in, so that the front faced the road. To Cale's surprise, the truck started and drove off. He knew Ray wasn't old enough to have a license, and his nonchalance in this lawbreaking was awe-inspiring. Cale figured that the Rowe parents were likely not there. Surely even they would not allow their underage kid to drive off in the family's only vehicle, if only for liability reasons.

Despite his intention of not getting any closer that day, he couldn't ignore the opportunity. Either no one was home and he could get an even better look, or it was just Lily there by herself now. If she was there, he could tell her he'd gotten lost in the woods and ask to use their phone. He didn't know if they had one, but that seemed like a reasonable opener. With the greatest threat gone, he got excited and started walking toward the shed. He kept it between himself and the downstairs back window to avoid revealing himself too soon.

"Hello?" he said quietly. A precaution, as he reached the shed. He waited. "Hello?" he said again, moving around to the front of it. He peeked in the door and saw only a wooden chair and some cardboard boxes on a shelf. He noticed a shovel and saw a hacksaw hanging on a nail, but no other tools or a lawn mower. That told him something, he felt, about what kind of people they were. He caught a whiff of something rank. A dead mouse maybe, he thought, or a few of them, though somehow more pungent. The smell kept him from lingering too long, and he held his breath for a moment and went up to the house. He gave a wave as he approached, though he couldn't see anyone inside. He went slowly up to the back door and peered through the busted screen and the smudged glass. In the kitchen, two of the cabinet doors were missing and one hung on one hinge. He scanned the room. The sink was full of dirty water. The peeling linoleum floor looked swept. He didn't notice the small table and chairs in the corner until Bonnie Rowe stood up and looked at him through the glass.

He felt himself scream silently. She seemed to look right through him, as if he weren't even there. He stepped back, stumbled.

"Sorry," he said. "Hi."

She opened the door and kept staring at him in that unsettling, removed way. Her brown hair was unwashed and messy, as if she'd just awoken. Up close, she looked younger than he'd expected, and her eyes were startling, a blue green, almost turquoise. It was well into afternoon, but she wore a thin white nightgown with small yellow flowers on it. Through a hole about the size of a quarter, he noticed a freckle on one of her large breasts.

"Is Lily home?" he sputtered. "I got lost in the woods."

She smiled skeptically and crossed her arms. She stared at his boots and looked him all the way up, taking so long that he wondered if she didn't hear him or couldn't understand, until she said, "She's working."

"Okay," he said.

"You're in her grade?"

"No," he said. "One higher. She's with my brother."

"So, what do you want from her?"

"I just got lost," he said, his nerves warbling his voice.

"I wasn't much older than her when I got Ray."

"Oh," he said. "I should go. I didn't mean to disturb you."

"What do you want with her?" she asked again.

"Nothing," he said. "Just, I got lost in the woods."

"You said that, but the road's right there."

"I was going to ask to use the phone. She's on my bus, so . . ."

"You want to come in and use the phone?"

"No, that's okay."

"You came up, looked in the house." She gestured for him to enter. "Why don't I show you the phone?"

"Actually, I know the way home."

Suddenly she grabbed his crotch. "I know what teenage boys want." She brought her face to his. She softened her grip but kept her hand there softly.

He pulled away, speechless and stunned.

"You got some balls coming up here." She slowly stepped out of the doorway onto the back step. Outside, she tucked two fingers into the waistband in the front of his jeans. "Let me see them." She pushed her fingers lower. "Look how hard you are."

He stammered and turned and ran, tripped and fell in the snow. Her taunting laugh followed him as he got up and stumbled past the shed. As he reached the big pine again, he paused and looked back at the house. She'd gone inside, but he could still hear the echo of her laughter. He was deeply embarrassed and still aroused. He thought about going back there and pounding on the door, but he didn't know whether he wanted to tell her off or tear open her nightgown.

The truck returned and he saw Ray and Lily get out, heard them talking. He bounded over the ridgeline and ran downhill as fast as he could, losing his footing and sliding onto his back in the snow. He got up again and ran along the bank, the snow melting in his boots. He crossed the bridge over Fox Brook but didn't stop until he reached the downslope of the smaller brook. There he laughed with relief, and suddenly aroused again, he jerked off into the snow, thinking of Bonnie Rowe's hand on him, and then he cried and went home in disbelief.

In the den, his mother was reading a book in the blue upholstered armchair. "You okay?"

"I don't feel well." He couldn't look at her.

"What's wrong?"

"Sick." He passed her and headed for the stairs.

"What are your symptoms, honey?"

"Too tired."

"Oh, no," she said. "That came on fast. I'll heat you up some soup. Is your stomach okay?"

"No."

When she brought him the soup he didn't want, he said, "Get that away from me. It stinks."

"I'll let you rest." She took the soup away. She brought up toast and ice water later, and he pretended to be asleep. She left it for him on the nightstand and tiptoed out.

That night, she asked to take his temperature with the mercury thermometer, but he refused. "It'll just take a minute." She laid the back of her hand against his forehead. "You don't feel feverish."

"Don't touch me," he snapped. "Just leave me alone."

She stepped back. She put her hands on her hips. He still couldn't look her in the eye. "Let's hope you feel better tomorrow," she said and left him alone.

Cale lay in the dark, with his eyes open, replaying in his mind the encounter with Bonnie Rowe. He knew it had happened, but it felt like maybe it hadn't. It was almost too preposterous to be real. He wondered who would even believe him, if he said anything. Not that so much had happened. She'd touched him, only for a moment. Filled him with a tingle and throb, terror and thrill. Somehow it made him want Lily even more. She resembled her mother, but she wasn't her. She embodied the excitement and danger, but she felt safer. He assumed that, like him, she was a beginner, and together they could learn things that would make her mother's touch seem like nothing.

11

Ambrose's mood was heavy when he cut his guys loose for lunch and climbed into his truck. Everyone was glad to get out of the cold wind and take a break from working double time to get ahead of the snow expected for the next day. But Ambrose had to go over to the Gindewins' house. He'd forgotten to take the diaper bag out of the truck, and Kate needed it. She was meeting with Harvey, who'd had a stroke last spring. His words had been taken from him by those things that take, is how Joan had put it. And now the sap was running again into the tin buckets nailed to the sugar maples along the roadsides, and soon the daffodils would push their green fingers up through the softening ground, but Harvey still hadn't said a word.

Kate had started working with him as soon as he was able. She was the speech therapist at Macoun elementary, as well as the librarian and one of two third-grade teachers. Her all-day nausea had been much worse with this second baby, and she'd gone on maternity leave earlier than initially planned. But no matter how bad she felt, she always kept her Tuesday appointment with Harvey, who'd quickly grown tired and frustrated with the exercises. He was never much of a talker anyway, was Joan's standing joke. Though, with a concerted effort, he was able to write brief notes on index cards and communicate some in that way. He remained mobile, too, and he'd started walking in the woods at night, Joan confided. When she asked him to stop, he wrote her a note that took a whole morning. He said it gave him peace, preparing for death.

"I used to think it was something in the water here," Joan said, as Ambrose entered with a soft double knock.

"Cursed, you mean?" Kate said, her voice low. She sat in the blue down-stuffed armchair by the kitchen fireplace, where the coals glowed. Sadie slept at her feet in the removable car seat with a dark-blue knit blanket draped over it. "Hey, Am."

"Hello, Ambrose." Joan sat in a straight-backed wooden chair. A mug of coffee steamed in front of her on the worn kitchen table. Her hair, more copper than silver still, was pulled back in a neat braid. She was in her late seventies, but she still walked miles every day at a good clip. She'd lived in Macoun her whole life and had never been gone longer than two weeks.

"Hi." Ambrose set the diaper bag within Kate's reach and stood by the door. "Where's Harvey?"

"Dining room, working," Joan said. "Coffee?"

"No, thanks," he said, relaxing slightly. "I need to get back to it."

Joan looked at Kate, resuming their conversation. "I don't mean cursed. I don't believe in that. I just mean, for such a small town, it feels like we've had more tragedy than most. But maybe it's all the same everywhere. I don't know."

Kate watched Sadie. "Maybe you just get to know people better in a small town. So you see more of their lives over the years than you would someplace big."

"Maybe," Joan said. "And yet, who do you know, really?"

"Well, I've only been here, what, five, six years? Not that Bellewood's much different."

"First, you don't know people," Joan said, "then you do, then you realize you don't."

"And then you do again?"

Joan laughed. "We'll see." She took off her glasses and wiped a lens, pinching it between a fold in her gray wool cardigan. "And maybe I'm just saying things because I'm used to talking for two." The old wide floorboards in the dining room creaked. "Speak of the devil," she said, without turning to see Harvey come in.

He emerged from the dim room. He wore brown suspenders clipped to blue jeans and a tan flannel shirt tucked in. Eyes down, bald spot in his close-cropped gray hair. Clean-shaven, chin nicked in two places and one more along his jaw.

"Your ears burning?" Joan said.

He grunted faintly and looked up. His eyes were different colors, one brown and one light blue. A scar ran down his cheek beneath the blue eye. Ambrose's breath snagged in his throat. Most kids he knew growing up were scared of Harvey. The startling eyes and the scar were part of it, but there was something else, too, that couldn't quite be named. Some kind of presence he had.

"We were getting tired of waiting on you, honey," Joan said. "Figured I'd draw you out."

They watched him as he made his way to Kate and handed her a note written on an index card. He sidled up to the counter, where he leaned, before opening a drawer.

"Harvey," Ambrose said, studying his own boots.

"I hope we'll get back to the exercises," Kate said. "I'm not helping much just reading these notes."

"Well, it's nice having you by, regardless," Joan said. "So, what's the news today?"

She read the note. "Says he found Abe." Her mouth opened and she looked at Ambrose in surprise, seemingly ready to laugh at the coincidence.

Joan shook her head. "He hasn't seen anybody."

Harvey pointed to the note.

"Abe, huh?" Joan said. "Abe who? And where?"

Harvey stared at Ambrose, who looked away and said, "I'll see you all later."

Joan grimaced and blushed. "You didn't even get anything to eat."

"I'm good. Nice to see everyone." He waved to Kate. "See ya at home."

"Be safe," she said, turning her attention back to Joan.

As he stepped outside, Ambrose heard Joan say softly, "Not him again, please. I swear, if it's him, you told me you were done with that."

Ambrose shut the door behind him and stood on the stone step. The sky was white with clouds too thin to cry, the same way it'd been, he remembered, the day his father missed the bend. He hit the only tree in a stretch of a hundred yards. A pale paper birch on the edge of a hayfield covered in a hard inch of snow. Seb Bainer's field, right down from the Rowes'.

That was Tuesday, March 9, 1993, days before the No Name Storm. And despite the chatter about the looming nor'easters, the road had been fine that morning, and his dad had driven it most of his life. A cautious man who always wore his seatbelt wasn't wearing a seatbelt, and his bumper grazed the tree's trunk enough to slam his chest against the steering wheel. And soon came the wailing of sirens, and the hospital, and the ICU. Lily Rowe had been home sick from school that day. If she hadn't, Ambrose knew, his father never would've had a chance. She's the one who called for help.

12

Lily pulled into the parking lot of the Valley offices to go meet with Gerlano. After the company party, she'd expected him to call to apologize, though she was glad that he never did. She didn't want to talk to him or anyone else about anything that'd happened. She had a job to do, and that was it. She'd resented being singled out for that meaningless award and paraded in front of everyone, embarrassed, asked to explain herself on the fly. She'd torn her gift certificate to shreds that night and let it flutter out the open window of her pickup on the way home.

At the office, she parked in a visitor spot. It was quarter to eight in the morning and she had a few minutes to kill. On the radio, the NPR correspondents were talking about record oil prices. Following its February 2022 invasion, the Russian army had begun murdering civilians in Ukraine, bombing hospitals and schools. This news brought a heaviness into her heart and worries to mind. She turned off the engine and stepped out into the parking lot, which was surrounded with ornamental crab apple saplings. They'd been planted the previous spring and girded with wiring to get them to grow straight. The weather had a cold edge, despite the sun. The night before, it had been warm and the rain had pounded so hard on her roof that she'd opened the front door to check for hail. It'd erased all the snow except for the big banks the plows had pushed up.

She approached the long two-story brown brick building. The company owned it and they were the only tenants now. Lily noticed more cars in the lot than she'd expected, more people. Though she spent almost all of her time in the field, she'd held meetings in the empty lot in the peak of the pandemic when most of the office crowd had shifted to remote work. Getting out of her truck, she felt self-conscious in her tan work boots, jeans, and flannel button-down. That was how she dressed every day, but the culture on a jobsite was different than in the office, and going in there always made her feel like she was back in school, where she'd never had clothes that hadn't drawn snickers. She passed Gerlano's new luxury SUV. She knew it cost more than twice her gross salary. It was one of several in his personal fleet. Each vehicle was customized with tough-guy features he'd never need, like chrome brush guards and bulletproof glass.

Entering the building, she waved to one of the security guys, Daniel Canfield, who'd flunked out of the police academy, apparently because of rage issues. He was known as a dangerous dope, a human bulldog with a crew cut who flew a giant flag behind his Bronco and had a few boneheaded arrests under his belt. An electrician had once told Lily that Canfield had gone to Bellewood High, and he got caught breaking into Kate Casey's house, no less. He left a love poem on her pillow that read like it'd been written by a third grader, the electrician said. Hearing that had made Lily feel sorry for Canfield, even though he'd never even bothered to acknowledge her. She knew that Gerlano had started using him here and there for little side projects. Gofering and private event security, which she understood was to test his loyalty and probably to groom a fall guy.

Canfield looked up from his phone at Lily and then looked back down.

"Hey," she said, without breaking stride, and he nodded. She took the stairs and went down the hallway to the corner office. Gerlano's secretary, Marcia, had been a teenage beauty queen many years before and still tried to play the part. She told Lily to have a seat.

"Hi, Marcia," she said.

"He'll be with you when he's with you."

Lily waited, nervous, still confused as to why Gerlano had called her in. It was like him to give no details. A promotion seemed unlikely, she thought, because he was cheap and liked to keep people where they were. She worried he'd dragged her over so he could apologize all this time later. She feared that, as part of his apology, he would ask her to talk about her family. She was almost certain now that he'd had somebody dig into her past already, and most likely before he'd hired her. She knew he often used private investigators. It made her wish she'd gone off to California or anywhere else a long time ago, though she couldn't have. Ray would come back someday, she felt. And there was his secret to protect, their secret. She waited.

After twenty minutes, Gerlano came out of his office, saying, "There she is." He was in his early fifties, short, slightly hunched. The way he moved was slow-footed but darting, like a spirited senior suddenly on the cruise ship dance floor. He wore a blazer over a lime-green golf shirt. His wiry, rust-colored hair was thinning, and she knew he combed it up throughout the day to add volume.

She shook his hand, noticing his jeweled fraternity ring and a gold bracelet.

"Can I get you anything, Lily? Coffee, water?"

"No, thank you."

"Marcia, get us some of the fizzy waters."

"Yes, boss," Marcia said, in a singsong way, with a forced and wrinkle-free smile.

He escorted Lily into the large office. The shades were down on the long windows. On one wall, she saw framed pictures of cars and of Frank smoking cigars, celebrating victories with local big shots and horses. He invited her to sit in one of two suede captain's chairs and he went to his standing desk. She couldn't see his face behind the flat-screen monitor.

"Nice boots," he said.

"A lot to do on-site still," she said.

"I'm kidding. Relax. You don't keep a pair of heels in your car?"

"No."

"It doesn't matter. Look, tell me what you know about Meryl Gibbs."

"From Macoun?"

"One of the biggest landholders in teeny-tiny little Macoun, yes."

"Beyond what I've been telling you since I started?"

"You haven't told me that much, believe me."

"I live just up the road from her."

"I know that," he said.

"I still think it could be a good investment when the time comes."

He leaned around the computer screen and pointed at her. "But did you know she's dead?"

She sat back in the chair. "No."

"Been dead for five or six weeks now, down in Florida."

"Oh, no."

"Almost no one knows," he said. "But me, and now you."

"That's too bad." She sighed. "What was she, in her nineties?"

"Eighty acres."

"Okay?"

"I've been in contact with her son for a while. He's an actor in Orlando. I guess he needed the money, after all, so . . ."

"You bought it?"

"Deed's in transit."

"That was my idea," she said.

"I heard you. I listened, because I'm an elegant modern man. And I looked into it myself, using my money. What do they say about talk again?"

"So it's like that?"

He stepped out from behind his workstation and waved his hand with a magician's flourish, painting a picture in the air, a distraction while he set up his next illusion, a trick. "I'm thinking a little upscale motel, restaurant, recreation facility, natural swimming experience. Rustic elegance. Fun, like a summer camp for adults, for New Yorkers who don't want to drive all the way to Vermont for fall foliage. What do you think?"

"That's more than I pitched you. Can't imagine it all fitting there right."

"Don't worry about that."

"That's what you want to put just down the road from me?"

"No, you're gonna put it down the road from you," he said. "Knowing that area like you must, I want you to run it. Break ground early fall. Big job, and I know you're the right person for it."

"Okay." She nodded, thinking. "We'll be done with the Res Shoppes end of summer."

"But first thing, I need you to get that waterway cleaned up." He stood at the window, looking out into the parking lot. "Dredge it and spread that crap on the banks so it has plenty of time to dry. We're still finalizing a couple things, but we've got the okay from the Gibbs guy to go in on account of it's good for him either way. Move quick and we can get ahead of some of the red tape with these local losers whining, dragging their heels. Nothing can kill you like water. The EPA, a bunch of money-grubbing scumbags, I swear to God."

"Knowing what it's like there, I'd say I'll need to pull an excavator, a dump, and call it four guys, from the Shoppes, and we're going full tilt." She noticed a streak of mud on her boot and tucked it behind the chair leg. "If I do that, we'll lose a day at least, probably two."

"No, that won't work." He turned away from the window. "You've already lost your lead on that one."

"So you want it done immediately, but without using any resources?"

"We do have money." He smiled, and she could tell he thought it was charming, despite his stubby cigar-stained teeth. "That still counts, right?" he said. "Anyway, probably better it's not our trucks and all that just yet. Keep a lid on it."

She thought more. "I know a guy who might work. His dad was the one got me thinking about construction from the start. Casey. I owe him one."

"And if not, then the next guy, or the next guy, I don't care," he said. "It just needs to be done quick, got it?"

"Yes."

"We're up against it."

"I said yes."

He laughed. "Well, did you know you'll be starting another project between the one you're on now and that one up there?"

"Is this the project you're just telling me about for the first time right now?"

"You're smart," he said. "Pretty straightforward reno, that one."

"That's what you say every time you hand me a new mess."

"You'll figure it out."

"Yes, boss," she said, mimicking Marcia, but frowning.

He pointed a finger at her again. "Today's Tuesday."

"I guess we're both smart."

"Dredge by next Wednesday, March sixteen, latest."

"We got concrete at the Shoppes that day."

"She's beginning to see the method in my madness."

"Am I?"

"So maybe you'll have to figure out a way to move a little faster then, right?"

She stood and prepared to leave, more relieved by the content of the conversation than nervous about the new jobs and timelines, though she'd already been working fourteen-hour days and six-day weeks for months.

"One more thing," he said.

She stopped. Her back to him.

"I have someone doing some recon for me on all this. She might come talk to you, and she might not."

"This is your snoop?"

"Hey, you never told me. Who'd you take to La Ristorante?"

She turned to him. "I hit my three-year mark in June." She waved her hands in the air, with a flourish, as he had. "I expect a raise of twenty percent or I'll get it somewhere else."

He shook his head. "You're something else, you know that?"

"I wish that were true," she said, pulling the door closed behind her.

13

Cale had to call Janelle four times before she agreed to see him again. He told her he'd made a mistake in the way he'd ended their relationship and he wanted to clear the air. She screened his calls and did not return them until he left a message saying maybe he'd just stop by her house.

Now they sat in black metal chairs outside a coffee shop on Kapahulu Avenue in Kaimuki. A maroon umbrella cast them both in shade. Midmorning, and the temperature was already well on its way to eighty. Waiting for the coffees, Cale had listened to a couple talk about a local news story. Someone had been murdered and encased in concrete in a garbage can. The two suspects were still on the loose. "Not for long," the woman said with a lilting local accent. "These days, camera on every light pole. Government read every text message."

Janelle was not interested in his retelling of this anecdote. Nor did she appear to be interested in him. Cale thought at first that maybe she was putting it on, but the more he tried to engage her in conversation, the clearer it became that, to her, seeing him was only a chore.

"You wanted me to tell you a secret," he said.

She looked up from her phone.

"My dad was in a car accident." It wasn't what he'd planned to say.

"Recently?"

"No," he said. "Twenty-nine years ago." He nodded. "Today. To the day."

"I'm sorry," she said. "That was most of your life ago?"

"Yes." And that response struck him. He'd never really considered how the trajectory of his life had bent from that moment in time. He'd only known the one way.

"Was he okay?" she asked.

He was in the ICU for a few days, Cale told her. The first two days and nights, he and Ambrose were there in the hospital. A dull and terrifying blur with some still life images in sharp focus. A cluster of shiny metal poles with hanging bags of fluids in different hues. A red stain on the edge of a white sheet on a gurney gliding past. Their mother standing vigil. If she slept at all, it was only a few minutes at a time. With heavy eyes, she assured them it would all work out. After a couple of days, though, she insisted that the boys needed a return to "normalcy," as she called it. At school, they could see their friends, and not get too far behind in their work, because Dad was tough and he was going to be okay. The road might be long, but they'd make it.

Joan Gindewin had picked the boys up from school the day of the accident and sped them over the mountain to the hospital. She drove them home from the hospital, too, and stayed over at their house that Thursday night. Friday morning, March 12, she woke them with a full breakfast of pancakes, bacon, and eggs. As they moved the food around their plates, she tried to entertain them with stories of their father as a boy. She'd babysat him for many years, before she was even a teenager. The work was more unpaid than not, starting when little Eli was a newly motherless child. She told his sons about the time their father stepped on a yellow jacket nest, the time he fell out of a tree, the time a horse bit him. The moral of each story was the same: their dad was tough and resilient. But it became clear quickly that these memories were not helping the kids, and she stopped. Getting them ready for the bus, she told them that she'd be there when they came home from school. She just had to run out to the store to stock up on some groceries. The coming storm was all anyone could talk about on the radio. It marked a breakthrough in weather-tracking technology, they said, though many remained skeptical. It was New England, after all, where weather could be volatile and big storms in March were nothing new.

Cale didn't absorb much that day in school. His friends carried on the same as always. Many were quick to forget the anguish of another amid their own problems. But people whispered. The kids cheered when the vice principal announced over the intercom the early dismissal in light of the impending superstorm. "Have a nice long weekend," he concluded. Class hadn't been dismissed yet when Cale walked out. No one was in the halls. The waxed floor reflected the fluorescent lights. The lights crackled and hummed. In his ears, the knock of his footsteps sounded hollow. Dazed, he wandered toward an exit, the side door, outside of which upperclassmen were allowed to smoke if they had parental permission. He avoided this area usually, but he didn't care anymore. He saw Ray Rowe standing there. When Ray saw Cale, he laughed. He laughed and pointed at him. Cale didn't know why, but he walked on. And then Ray said, "You get what you deserve, you motherfucker. You little cocksucker." Cale kept going, feeling as if he were floating, thinking only of his dad and the wreck.

The morning of the accident he'd continued to make a point of giving only one-word responses to his father, of being cold. "Rude," his mother had said, a continuation of the behavior that had begun after Lily had infected him with an idea he couldn't shake. A sense of phoniness and disgust. A number of disparate feelings made more confusing by what had happened between him and Bonnie Rowe, with his firsthand knowledge of what she might do, of how she could be terrifying and attractive.

As he approached the school bus, he saw Lily standing by its door. She moved toward him. In her eyes, he saw little flashes of light. Her chin trembled. "I'm sorry about your dad," she said. "I hope he's okay."

"Is it true what you said?" he said. "About him and your mom?"

"No," she said. "I'm sorry. I was just trying to scare him off."

"Why?"

"Because he's a good man, and we're no good."

Cale blurted out, unthinking, "I love you," and then he climbed up the steps and took a seat halfway down the aisle. That was the second time they'd spoken, and in his derangement, he'd confessed a love based on very little, he felt. Based on a strange sense of truly knowing someone somehow, though he didn't really know her at all. The girl, it turned out, who'd led him incorrectly to distrust his own father. Such was her quiet power over him. He barely noticed Ray pass him in the aisle, laughing still.

When Ambrose got on the bus, looking vacant and hurt, Ray yelled, "Oh, look! It's the crash test dummy's other son!" Cale felt an immediate shock and turned to see Ambrose's stunned expression turn to one of gnarled rage. Teeth clenched, his brother stomped down the aisle to Ray.

"Shut your mouth!" Ambrose said.

"What're you gonna do, huh?"

"Shut your goddamn mouth or I'll shut it for you!" No one in Macoun had ever challenged Ray like that. The bus driver stood up and yelled for Ambrose to sit down.

As Cale told this story, Janelle's phone vibrated, rattling on the metal tabletop.

"Do you want to get that?" he asked, startled.

"Uh, it's fine," she said. "You can keep going. I do have a call coming up in a minute, though."

He shook his head and tried to continue with an abridged version. He said that Seb Bainer cut that birch tree down the day after his father hit it, as soon as Harvey Gindewin gave the okay. He cut it as close to the ground as he could, and he bucked it and put the rounds through the splitter until they were small enough for the chipper, which he aimed into a thicket out of sight.

That's why, when school was dismissed early, as the storm gathered, squeezing its pressure into his sinuses, Cale didn't see that tree through the bus window. He'd dreaded passing it. He'd expected police tape and shattered glass. But there was none of that. The tree was just gone, and only its absence remained.

Past the field, the bus turned around at the top of Waquaheag Road and began its descent toward the Rowes' again, where it would stop to let them out on their side of the road. Ray left the back seat and sat down right behind Ambrose. Cale turned to listen.

"I'm glad your dad's gonna die," Ray whispered. "You should've seen him sucking air like a fish. Come out today to my pond again, tough guy, and I'll smash your face in worse than his."

Cale wasn't sure he'd heard it right. It was too outrageous to process in a moment. But he saw Ray stand and walk down the aisle as the bus hissed to a stop. The levered door squeaked open. Ray turned and smiled at Ambrose.

Cale noticed his brother's body stiffen, seemingly locked, his face pale. He did not ask him what was the matter. He watched Lily, who gave him a wave. But when Ambrose stepped off the bus at their house, he dropped his backpack by the mailbox and turned right, on a dead march for the path through the woods.

"Where are you going?" Cale shouted to him.

"Fishing," he said, barely audible.

"Everything's iced over."

Ambrose said nothing. Their dog, Sammy, came out of the garage and bounded after him.

"You don't have a pole," Cale said. Ambrose didn't respond again. Cale jogged after him and grabbed his wrist as they reached the edge of the field. "What's with you?" Ambrose jerked his arm away hard. He turned to walk on, but then he paused. He looked at Cale, his eyes aflame, and he repeated exactly what Ray Rowe had said to him.

"You can't pretend you didn't hear him now," he said and walked on. Cale stood there, struck dumb, and then he followed his brother, slowly at first, as the words filled in and flooded. He didn't want to go, but he knew Ambrose wouldn't stop, and he had to have his brother's back.

At the coffee shop with Janelle, Cale leaned back in his chair and released a breath from so deep inside him it made a faint groaning sound, like the hinge on an old door opening. He felt drained, and yet he wasn't finished.

"This Ray sounds like a bad guy," she said.

"He probably never had a chance," Cale said. "But, yes. I would agree."

"I hate bullies," she said, standing. "If there was a fight, I hope your brother won."

"I just talked too much, didn't I?" He looked down.

"You're fine," she said. "I just have calls. I'm late."

"Can I take you out for dinner again? Somewhere real nice?" He gave a half-hearted wink that she didn't see as she looked at her phone again.

"I don't think so, Reese."

"Please," he said. "You can call me Cale."

"What?" Her forehead furrowed.

"That's my name. My real name, anyway. That's who I really am, I guess."

"Oh," she said. "Your name's not Reese?"

"My name's Caleb Reese Casey, but people always called me Cale."

"Okay?"

"You knew that."

"No, I think I'd know if I knew that."

"It's my middle name." He stood and clasped his hands in a pleading gesture. "But Reese isn't who I really am. I mean, professionally it is, but . . . There's more I should tell you. Maybe another time?"

She nodded then and puffed out her cheeks. "I wish you all the best, okay?"

"Can I call you? I'll wait, a few days, a week, a month. You tell me."

"I don't think it's good idea," she said. "I told you where I am. I'm not looking for someone to fix at this point, you know?"

"There's no fixing me," he said.

"I believe you."

"I mean, you don't have to fix me."

"I know," she said. "I don't have to fix you. It's not on me to fix you."

"Yeah."

"I had fun," she said. "And ultimately, I thank you for being honest with me before we went too far down the line, okay?"

"I'm being more honest with you right now."

"Well, honestly, it's too late."

He'd expected her to ask more, or be shocked, he didn't know. Here he was, saying things he'd never said, preparing to bare his soul, maybe, in a way he never had, sharing details many therapists and school psychologists had failed to get out of him. He'd anticipated a number of responses from Janelle, but boredom had not been one of them. He'd bored her, and now he felt embarrassed.

"I'll see you around, alright?" she said. "You know how the real estate world is here. Maybe we'll do a deal someday soon." She forced a smile and then walked away quickly, as if he might try to follow her. He sat down and put his head in his hands. It was just a conversation, a coffee. It was nothing, and yet he felt oddly devastated, in a way he hadn't since he was fourteen.

14

Ambrose drove to the site where he was building a country house for an anesthesiologist from New Haven. He focused on what needed to get done, the tangible tasks. Concrete and wood and steel. Snow was coming. He could feel it in the heavy air. The rises and falls in the road did not enter his upper mind. The three guys he'd managed to get working for him on this one wouldn't be there yet. Though the weather concerned him, he was glad he'd have some time to himself. He liked the quiet to map out the job in his mind, before the air was filled with banging and the beeping sounds of things in reverse.

A seam in the clouds opened as he turned into the long gravel driveway where the build was underway. The sun broke its yolk over the pines in his rearview. The truck crested a knoll and came around a bend, and where he expected simply a still life of yellow machines around a hole in the ground, he found a black pickup in the center of his tableau. He slowed. The truck's door opened and out stepped Lily Rowe. Ambrose felt his guts stew. "This town," he muttered to himself. He'd often bemoaned how the size of Macoun caused you to run into the same people and have the same conversations too often, but he'd never moved away, and he couldn't remember the last time he'd said a word to Lily. He pulled up and parked past her truck. He opened his glove box in search of nothing in particular.

"Lily Rowe," he said through the partly open window.

"Hi, Am." She came up beside him. "Looks like your foundation's all dug."

"Almost."

"Nice weekend, right? You believe it's supposed to snow all day, and melt away again tomorrow?"

"That's March, for now anyway, I guess," he said. "What can I do for you?"

"I got an opportunity for ya." She stood so close that he couldn't open the door without asking her to move, which he didn't. She removed an elastic from her wrist and pulled her hair back tight.

"You do?" he asked. "Or your boss does?"

"You don't like him?"

"Don't know him really. Just those big signs."

"The offer's mine," she said. "He doesn't care how I do it, as long as I get it done. And since we've known each other so long, I came to you first." She smiled. She had small straight teeth. Canines more pointed than most, which gave her an animalistic quality that he'd appreciated in other women when he was younger. She said, "You know how to dredge?"

He shut the glove box and popped the driver-side door open. She stepped back. Stomach acid pushed up into his throat. Seeing her always produced in him this same sick feeling, even when he was prepared. In high school, seated between a campfire and a thirty-pack of Bud, Ambrose had said once or twice that he feared no one, and that was almost entirely true. He'd done two years of college, still living at home, and in the wildness of his youth, many guys had tried him and gotten knocked out. Once, an aspiring mugger in Hartford's north end pulled a knife on him and Ambrose put the guy in the hospital with a left hook that dropped his head to the curb. He'd only frozen in one fight in his life, and he'd been in many after that to prove to himself it would never happen again. But Lily Rowe still had his number. She was living proof that he was living a lie, he knew. A lie that put his family in jeopardy, even when he was able to forget for a while. And then he'd pass her at the gas station or at the town dump and spend hours thinking about her brother, her father, and of course his own.

"Don't know if you heard," she said. "But Meryl Gibbs passed away."

Ambrose failed to hide his shock. "I just saw her."

"Sad, yeah." She nodded and dragged the toe of her boot through the dirt. Then, softening her tone, speaking slowly and gently, she told him how Gerlano had bought the land. Ambrose felt like he was hovering over the conversation, not quite there. He was processing only bits. A stream of information he found relentless.

"You in or what?" she said. "I need to move quick. Think you and your crew want to take a break here and lend a hand?"

"Do what now?" he said.

"We're gonna dredge Gibbs Pond. Make it deeper. Make it good again."

"Dredge?"

"You know, dig it out," she said. "Make it nice. I don't know if it's work they were doing upstream, but apparently it's not flowing like it did, not like I remember. A lot of silt built up, I think."

He wiped his hands across his forehead and face. "It's plenty nice as it is."

"You gotta get all that crap out early to let it dry."

"It's not even spring yet."

"Sure, there'll be rain," she said. "But scheduling. We're a little overextended at the moment and it's only gonna get worse. I mean, look, I'll just tell you the truth. Gerlano can be a real pain in the ass, and it's always more, more, more."

"So say no."

"Yeah." She appeared unconvinced. "Anyway, offer is, if you can get it done in a week, I'll pay a double day rate. My drop-dead's next Tuesday, the fifteenth." A lone Canada goose called out from the sky, out of sight.

"I'm a little lost here," Ambrose said.

"I know you're still just getting going, so I figured some quick easy money could be okay, on account of we're friends, no? Definitely more opportunities to be had, once we prove you out."

"About the pond," he said. "The land, I mean. That can't be right, right?"

"Deed's in transit. Been a long time coming too. Soil scientists and the wetlands people, all looking good. You know her son?"

He leaned back against the truck, his legs wobbly.

"You alright?" She eyed him.

"Maybe," he sputtered. "I got food poisoning."

"Oh no," she said. "That's awful. What'd you eat?"

He closed his eyes.

"Sorry. You probably don't want to talk about food."

His stomach turned. He put his fist to his mouth. He tried to choke it down. He stumbled around the back of the truck and moved toward the tree line beyond the dirt, hoping to salvage some semblance of dignity, of privacy, secrecy, anything. But he couldn't and he didn't, and in plain view, he did something he hadn't done since he was a kid. He puked.

He puked, as he had on the bank of Gibbs Pond all those years back while the first flurries of the big storm fell, and the boy's blood leeched into the white ground, and Cale cried, *We can't do this to Mom. We can't do this to Mom.*

15

After talking to Ambrose, Lily drove home and sat on her bed, still in her work clothes, running through the rest of the week in her mind. She'd learned to view each day as a punch list. A series of tasks to complete as efficiently as possible, always moving on to the next action. That's how she planned to get promoted by summer, and land a more senior role at a bigger developer in Fairfield County by the fall. That courtship had begun already, and in three years, she planned to have her own company, which would poach Gerlano's top clients and talent. In ten years, she thought, she will have buried him. The Gibbs project, though, caused her to reconsider this timeline. She was sick of her boss and had outgrown her role, but she felt this one could be a centerpiece project for her. And the initial idea had been hers. With the opportunity, of course, came the risk. If the end product did what she knew it could, who would that attract to the area? Who would come along next and start poking around in places best left undisturbed?

She sat up on the bed. She had one piece of art on the wall, a framed poster from the Bob Dylan movie *Don't Look Back*. She liked his music more than anyone's, but that message had meant more to her than any song. She'd seen the poster in the window of a junk shop when she was sixteen. Though she'd never liked spending money, she paid what felt like an exorbitant sum for it then, forty bucks. That poster led her to the music, rather than the other way around, and that title, that line, had become an organizing principle of her life. In the past, she'd been weak. She'd had no control. But those days had ended with her father.

She got up from the bed and put her boots in the closet. On the top shelf, she had a black duffel bag packed with essential items. Warm water-resistant clothes, nonperishable food, ten grand in cash, in case the day came when she had to run again, like when she was a kid. She had a notebook in there too. Ray's. And though it went against her beliefs about the past, she made the exception for her brother. Once in a while, when she was missing him most, on holidays or one of their birthdays, she'd take down the notebook and read Ray's plan for their future. It'd been part of a school assignment he'd never turned in. In his messy handwriting, with nearly half the words misspelled, he laid out the vision he'd told her about. The two of them, in Alaska, living off the land together. Answering to no one. Safe.

She shut the closet and went into the living room, crossing the same floor where Ray had found their father passed out all those years before. That was early February of 1993, when Ray had given their mother another sleeping pill crushed up in a glass of water. He then went out to the shed and got a cinder block, which he lifted high and threw down, cracking the narrow wooden floorboards there, and smashing his father's skull. He did it again, and again. He mopped up the blood and brain poorly with old towels and dragged the body out to the shed. When Lily crept back to the house after hiding from her father in Seb Bainer's hayloft, she checked it out covertly from the edge of the woods. She saw Ray driving their father's truck, forward and reverse, forward and reverse, in front of the house.

Ray had been acting strange, especially since he'd been thrown against the railing. He'd spent that night vomiting. Concussed, Lily assumed, though they didn't go to the doctor. "Doctors is a waste of money," Abe Rowe often said. After that incident, though, Ray started sleeping out more in the cave above Gibbs Pond, despite the cold. Lily understood that he just couldn't take it anymore. And something seemed to have jarred loose, she believed later. But seeing him driving the truck that day told her there was no immediate danger. Their father must've gone off, because he would not have allowed that. When she approached the house, Ray hopped out of the truck and ran up to her, giddy.

"I have a surprise for you," he said, bouncing with excitement.

In the two days she'd hid out, she'd drunk rainwater from a bucket and eaten only half a pack of old chewing gum she'd found in one of Seb's greasy jackets. Her stomach felt hollowed out and ached. She was exhausted from shivering, and the night before, she'd become so weary from hunger and sleeplessness that she was pretty sure she'd hallucinated. She thought the shadows on the wall were saying things, telling her she was okay.

Returning home, she was thrilled by Ray's excitement, believing there had to be food. He led her into the house. Maybe Mr. Casey had brought something more, and better, she hoped. She had the idea of a pie, an apple pie. But she quickly understood something was off. Ray was too happy, flitting around. He wasn't acting right. Then she saw what she thought at first was dried mud smeared on the floor.

"We're going out there." Ray pointed through the window to the shed.

"Ray, what is this?"

"You ready to see something amazing?"

"Ray?"

"Lily." He took her by the shoulders. "Don't you get it? You're free." He led her out to the shed, telling her not to worry, but she trailed behind him nervously. What she found was sickening. He hadn't talked to her before doing it. He'd just gone ahead with it, without a plan, and she was shocked into this new reality. She kept her eyes averted from the bloody mess of a head, but that didn't spare her from seeing that Ray also had cut the right hand from their father's body. She saw the ragged stump of a wrist, two bones like broken teeth jamming out of plum meat.

"My God, what'd you do?" She retched and looked at the rotted plywood floor. The rancid stink was thick.

"You're free," he said again.

"You cut off his hand?"

"You want the other?" Ray asked, wonder in his voice. "We can each have one, like a trophy." She stumbled backward and fell onto the ground outside of the shed. Shaking, she scrambled to her feet and took off running.

"Don't be a baby," Ray called out. Her reaction of horror and sadness clearly disappointed him. She ran down the road and into the field, where she stopped. She couldn't breathe. She was sucking air, hyperventilating. She felt dizzy. She thought she was going to faint or die. She put her hands on her knees. A school counselor somewhere had once told her about deep breathing, and she focused on that. Counting, as she inhaled, and exhaled. She continued to do this as she began aimlessly walking laps around the perimeter of Seb Bainer's field, still feeling sick and sad and panicked, all the while trying to convince herself that this was a good thing, like Ray said. A necessary thing. Self-protection. Her most dangerous threat had been neutralized, bringing a whole new set of dangers, of which Ray appeared oblivious.

As the sun set, she sat against the birch tree on the edge of the field, thinking, and then she returned to the shed. Her brother had the body rolled up in the tarp that'd been tied down over them during all those moves from state to state.

"You're not gonna tell on me, right?" he said.

The answer was, of course, no, and she told him that they needed to take their father way out into the woods and bury him, and then leave in the pickup, once and for all, headed west.

Ray agreed that they needed to get rid of the body. Together, they rolled it onto a splintering toboggan Lily took from Seb Bainer's barn. She also borrowed two shovels, and by the light of a nearly full moon, she found a low spot deep in the woods between two swales, and they started to dig. Hacking through the frost layer proved difficult, and Ray quit after they'd reached a depth of six inches.

"Let's just burn him," he said.

"With what?" she said. "Besides, what if someone finds the spot."

Ray watched her work for another hour. "It's deep enough."

"No, it's not," she said.

Similar exchanges continued.

"This is why you have a plan," she eventually snapped. "A schedule, communication. Or better yet, you don't do this at all."

"I'm bored with this," he said. "I'm going back." And he left her to finish the job he'd pulled her into. But there was no going back now, she felt, and she couldn't imagine receiving any pity from a jury or judge, in general. She understood, too, that the missing hand undercut the genuine claim of their self-defense.

As Lily dug deeper, the work became a little easier, despite the rocky terrain. She'd reached about four feet by the time she began to hear the first birds of the morning, and then she pulled the tarp with all her remaining strength and rolled the body into the hole. She closed her eyes and worked quickly, pushing the piles of dirt in, wanting to see no more. She walked on the grave to tamp it down, and as a final touch she moved a few rocks on top and used a branch to sweep snow over it. It didn't look right, but she could do no more.

Walking home, shivering, her clothes filthy and stiff from frozen sweat, she worried about Ray. Over the next few days, certain changes in him became even more pronounced. He was more relaxed than he'd ever been. He even returned to school and caused no trouble for weeks, a month. The paraeducator who shadowed him all day stopped Lily in the hallway one day to say how well he'd been doing. He seemed to have turned over a new leaf, she said.

Still, Lily had a hard time looking at him. The thrill of the killing for Ray, the adrenaline or whatever it was, didn't seem to dissipate. It appeared to be all upside to him, light and bright. His only regret, he told her, was waiting so long. He wished he'd killed the old man many years before.

He suggested other ways he should've done it, strangling him with an extension cord, taking an axe to his throat. Lily wept for their father. She wept for the things that had made him the way he was. She couldn't make sense of Ray's reaction. She worried.

But she waited anyway for good weather so they could make their escape. She didn't know then that Ray had cut off their father's other hand, too, when she'd been out pacing in the field, and he'd kept them both as souvenirs, rotting in a plastic bag. He'd hidden them from her in the shed.

Later, she knew that Mr. Casey had seen her brother playing with those hands on the front steps of their house, the day in March when he crashed into the tree. The man had disregarded or never received her warning, and then he'd come once more bearing groceries, bringing charity, and he'd seen something no one should have. And if he hadn't, who knows?

16

Cale had passed out enough times in the old days to remember "passing in," waking up, usually confused. After his coffee with Janelle, he went to Uncle Ling's bar on Kapahulu when they opened for lunch and sat there dazed behind a martini, watching the blades of the ceiling fan spin slowly. The place was empty, and he felt the same way. His phone vibrated in his pocket. When he looked at it, he didn't immediately recognize the number. It was very rare now that he ever saw the 860 area code on an incoming call, though the robo-dialers had gotten more sophisticated with their tricks, he thought. Then it occurred to him who was calling. He didn't have his brother's number saved. The silence between them predated cell phones, but then it just snapped into focus.

He came to and ignored the call. What did Ambrose want after all this time, he wondered. But in his mind, Cale was already following him again through the woods to

Gibbs Pond. He saw their dog, Sammy, running off ahead. The snow had melted and frozen into a hard crust underfoot. Overhead, the churning storm sky pressed down. They followed the brook under a bridge and across the cow pasture. At the edge of the field, they crawled under the electric fence and the barbed wire, and they entered into the woods that were owned by Meryl Gibbs. They passed over the rise where they'd stopped with their dad the day Ray had shot an arrow at them, the last time the Caseys had gone fishing. They didn't see any sign of Ray when they got to the pond, which was still frozen over, though thinning from a recent thaw. Ambrose called out to him, his anger undiminished. Cale's own frustration and fury about what Ray had said was waning. He didn't have Ambrose's temper, and he was mostly relieved when it seemed no one else was there. He'd begun to believe it was all a bluff. An empty cruelty from a damaged kid.

"Let's go home," Cale said. "Missus Gindewin's gonna worry, and Mom."

Ambrose yelled, "Here I am, Ray! You hiding now?"

"Come on, Am. Please. He's not here." He looked around for the dog. "Sammy, come!" He kept calling for her. Several minutes passed. The thumping blood in Cale's ears softened and slowed. A heavy dread sank into his stomach. He called for Sammy again, and then they heard a sharp yelp from up on a ledge across the water, followed by the loud broken whimpering that told them a dog was in real pain.

Ambrose raced toward the sound, across the thin ice, sliding and not lifting his feet. Cale shouted for his brother to be careful, but soon Ambrose was scrambling up the hillside and onto the boulders, toward the steeper ledges that overlooked the pond. Hesitant again, Cale followed him across the ice, which creaked under his weight. He'd always feared falling through a hole in the ice and being unable to find his way out of the water again, trapped. But he made it to the bank and climbed, gaining on Ambrose. The dog's whimpering had slowed and quieted by the time Cale got up on the ledge right behind his brother.

There, they found Sammy, twisting and writhing, her forelegs under her belly, her back legs pushing her body around in rough dragging circles, staining the snow in red and rust. An arrow stuck out from the side of her chest, a deer hunter's heart shot just missed. Her pale fur was matted with blood. Ray Rowe stood over her with his bow. He watched her with a distant smile, transfixed. He looked up at the Casey brothers with what appeared to be surprise, and then the smile grew, and there was a flash of rage that detonated Cale's mind white. In an instant, as the world materialized around him again, he saw Ambrose charging Ray.

Cale's phone vibrated again on the bar at Uncle Ling's, and he spooked, nearly knocking over the martini he hadn't touched. He was relieved to see it wasn't Ambrose calling again but rather his assistant, Derek.

He answered.

Derek said, "They're waiting for you."

"Who?"

"Well, Mister Igashi and your prospective client."

"Shit, I'll be right there." Cale had forgotten that he'd set a lunch meeting with a software exec who was test-driving agents. She was looking to buy a house in the low eight figures, and he had a handful of swanky listings in Portlock and Kahala. Picking up both sides on one of those commissions would give his spirit a boost, he knew. His plan had been to use this client to seal the deal on being made a partner in the firm. But his usual laser focus had drifted.

He put a twenty on the bar and raced out into blinding light. He pulled his Wayfarer sunglasses from the front pocket of his blue aloha shirt and stepped quickly into the street. A moped driver had to swerve to avoid him, nearly veering into oncoming traffic in the opposite lane. The moped wobbled but straightened out and traveled on slowly. The driver of a car that'd nearly hit the moped laid on the horn. Cale waved and crossed the street in front of it. The horn didn't stop until he was pulling the door open at Ono, sweating. The stains under his arms were bigger than he could hide. He took a breath, reminded himself how many deals he'd closed before.

He was trying to come up with a good excuse for why he was late. But in his mind, he saw Ambrose tackling Ray Rowe, who went down on the rock ledge and wheezed as the air was slammed from his lungs. Ambrose landed on top, but Ray grabbed a handful of his hair and pulled his head sidewise. In one deft move, Ray slid out from underneath and pinned him.

"Am!" Cale squeaked. "Am!"

Ray laid his forearm across Ambrose's throat and began laying down pressure, staring into his eyes, seeming to savor the breathless terror on Ambrose's face. With his knees, he held Ambrose's arms to the ground. Ray sprinkled some of the hair he'd ripped from Ambrose's head onto his face and laughed some more, toying with him. Cale was immobile, stiff with fear.

"You should've listened, tough guy," Ray said. "Don't you see? You're powerless."

Cale walked into the conference room at Ono Real Estate. His CEO, Glen Igashi, sat at one end of the long table and Derek sat several seats away, jotting notes. The scratching of his pen was the only sound in the room. On the table, three glass vases held orchids and black roses. Cale had asked his florist and the decorator he used for staging houses to make the space look exotic and singular. A sushi chef had set up a workstation against the wall behind the table, and he stood with his arms crossed.

"She left," Glen said, the annoyance clear in his voice. He was a big man, kind. "Fluffy," peopled called him. A numbers guy who paid careful attention to detail, except when it came to his clothes.

"She couldn't wait five minutes?" Cale asked.

"It was twenty."

"No way."

"I called you, sir," Derek said.

"What, one minute ago?"

"I didn't want to disturb your important coffee," he said. "How was it?"

"Not now, Derek." Cale shook his head and sat down.

Glen said, "She said she had other meetings."

"Was she pissed?"

"We're not getting her business. I think that's for sure."

"Sorry. I'll call her. I'll fix it. I'll try to fix it."

"Are you alright?" Glen said. "You've been slipping lately."

"I'm fine." Cale's phone vibrated again and he took it from his pocket.

"Is it her?" Glen asked, with a sudden hopeful look.

"No, it's my brother." He ignored the call again.

"How long have I known you?" he said. "I didn't know you had a brother."

"I don't," Cale said. "Someone must've died."

17

Ambrose hung up when his call went to Cale's voicemail again. He opened another beer in his cold truck. The snow had started a little after eight that Wednesday morning, blowing up and down and sidewise in a swirling wind. It came on fast and didn't quit.

Ambrose had bumped around at work in a haze that day. He was still staggered by his conversation with Lily the afternoon before. A few times, one of his guys asked if he was feeling alright, and he said he was fine. They worked for an hour in the snow that morning, stiff and puffed up like birds, until Ambrose said they'd call it a day. He kept working, though, and he knew they were watching him through their windshields.

Even after they left, he walked around through the snow, moving quickly, accomplishing nothing. He spent hours like that, his mind spinning, without clarity or direction, until four inches covered the places he hadn't been. His unlined leather gloves were soaked through to his numb hands. The cold went well down into him, into his bones. Instead of a late lunch, he picked up a twelve-pack of beer and sat in his truck on the side of an untraveled road, staring at his phone, wondering what to do.

And now it was night and he was parked again, just down the road from Lily's. He hadn't gone home yet. Kate had put Sadie to bed alone. The second night in a row that'd happened, after two years during which he'd never missed her bedtime routine.

The night before, he'd knocked on Lily's door, startling her. He'd come to tell her that, after careful consideration, he was eager to accept the job dredging Gibbs Pond. His acceptance, he'd decided, couldn't wait until the morning. She was surprised to see him, and, he felt, disappointed. She said she'd hired someone else already. She hadn't thought Ambrose was interested, and perhaps he wouldn't be well enough to do the work on time, on account of his food poisoning or stomach bug or whatever it was. He let his desperation show, offering to do the job for free, just him, no crew needed. When she asked why he'd do that, he mumbled "never mind" and stepped off the porch. She stepped outside then and asked if he agreed that the job required two people, bare minimum, given the need for a dump truck, as well as the excavator, but even that would likely be insufficient, and at the very least inefficient. His response was to fade off into the night without a goodbye or closing comment.

But a day later, he had an answer for why he'd made that offer, why it had to be him. Doubling down on his initial half-baked pitch, he got out of his truck and walked along the edge of the field that he knew too well. The wet snow squeaked and groaned under each step. The flakes falling were barely visible now. He could hear them sizzle on his collar, melting on impact, even with his pulse pounding in his ears.

He took a breath and knocked on her door again. Lily appeared less surprised this time, but more puzzled. She wore a t-shirt and black satin pajama pants. "You been drinking, Am?" she asked. Behind her, the house was spotless, spartan. The TV flickered, mute.

"No," he said. "Look, that land, Gibbs Pond, it's special to me. I used to play there as a kid, and fish. My family. So if there's no way around digging it up, it needs to be someone who'll do it with care. Respect. Meryl would've wanted it that way."

"I got Wheeler."

"They're no good."

"I thought Joe was your friend."

"He is. I didn't mean it like that. Just, I should do it. Can you just tell him you decided to go another direction?"

"I don't think so."

He tried to charm her. "Please?"

"I already put in a down payment."

"Why would you do that?"

"We're moving on this. I don't have time to play patty-cake."

"I'll talk to Joe."

"Do what you're gonna do," she said. "But hey, I don't need any extra drama, know what I mean? I'll get you on the next one."

"No drama here," he said.

"Knocking on my door two nights in a row. I got a phone too, you know?"

"Sorry," he said. "I don't have your number. But that land. It's just, the land."

She studied him. "If I didn't know better, I'd think you wanted me to invite you inside."

Half drunk for courage, he considered that. "I should get home."

"Yeah, you say hi to your wife for me," she said. She began to close the door but stopped, adding, "And say hi to your brother."

He turned quickly and bumped against the railing. In the truck, he slammed the steering wheel with his palms. He squeezed it as hard as he could, throttling it, screaming with his mouth closed. "Fucking Ray Rowe," he said, punching the gas hard. The tires squealed and the truck thumped onto the road, fishtailing in the snow.

In that moment, Ambrose remembered being pinned on the ledge overlooking Gibbs Pond, when he'd felt himself beginning to fade. Ray had pressed his elbow harder against his throat. Ambrose closed his eyes with the pain and pressure. That's why he didn't see Cale crash in, driving a shoulder into Ray's jaw, knocking him onto his back. At the edge, Ray didn't appear afraid at all. He lay there for a moment, his head dangling over the cliff lip, looking at the treetops, which would've appeared upside down from his angle. He moved his jaw slowly side to side, testing it.

"Sorry," Cale said. Ambrose rolled over and got to his feet, gasping. He rubbed his throat. Cale said, "You shot our dog." His voice cracking. Sammy had stopped circling and lay on her side, panting. "You shot our dog." On the brink of tears, an accusation and a plea at once.

Ray slowly sat up. He shook his head but remained silent. His chin to his chest, his eyes glaring up at them. Ambrose looked at the bow in the snow beside him as Ray got to his feet. He seemed to reconstitute himself on the edge of the cliff, to regain strength, to grow. He darkened and warped. Ambrose felt as if they'd just encountered a demon. Later, he rationalized this feeling as something caused by stress, the choking, which would've affected the oxygen to his brain. And yet a fear like he'd never known entered him. In a frenzy, he scanned the snow for an arrow.

"No," Ray said, with effort. "I killed your dog. And now I feel like killing you."

Ray moved toward them, cutting off their angle of escape. He backed them up until they were cornered against the rock face.

"We're just gonna go home," Cale said, his voice sharp and wavering.

Ray shook his head no.

"Please," Cale said.

Ray laughed at him. That's when Cale screamed and rushed him. Ray clawed at him, got his fingernails into the sides of Cale's neck and wrenched his head to the side. Ray was about to put him into a headlock, but Cale stepped left and got free enough to hit the older boy in the chin with a slashing elbow. Ray's head and his hair and his arms flung back. Eyes wide and white, he stumbled backward and slipped and then they saw the soles of his boots and he was gone.

Stricken, they looked over the edge and saw Ray's body lying on the bank of Gibbs Pond, arms bent, legs splayed. His head cranked unnaturally to the side, neck twisted. Even from that height, they could see the snow all around his head, how the red wept into the white.

"He's okay," Cale said. "He's okay." He began to cry. "He's okay." He looked back over the ledge once more, and then burst out sobbing. "We can't do this to Mom. We can't do this to Mom." He repeated it and repeated it, and it became a broken mantra. Ambrose thought of their mother waiting for their father outside the ICU, and those words, spoken or not, became all he heard. They became the rhythm to the work as he used a rock to smash through the ice. The water pressed up from the hole and spread out along the edge and wet his knees, so cold he couldn't feel them. His jeans froze. He kicked snow over the blood. *We can't do this to Mom.* The words echoed as each boy grabbed one of Ray Rowe's arms and dragged him toward the hole, their eyes averted, unable to look. *We can't do this to Mom.*

They packed rocks into Ray's clothes as best they could, and then they pushed him into the hole with their feet pressed against his. The ice bowed slightly under the weight but didn't break. The body slid into the water effortlessly, with no splash or resistance, like a seal slipping back under the surface.

Ambrose said, "We have to get Sammy." His voice came from some distant place, as if it were someone else speaking. "They could connect it."

"I killed him," Cale said on the bank, hugging his knees to his chest. "I killed him?"

"It was an accident," Ambrose said. "It was self-defense. He killed himself." And alone, Ambrose climbed the ledge. Losing his footing frequently, he carried down the now almost silent dog in his arms. Her blood soaked his tan coat. They said goodbye to her with tears streaming down their cheeks and their bodies convulsing and the snow really coming down now. Ambrose pulled the blunt metal arrow from Sammy's side and carried her out onto the ice. The temperature was dropping fast and a thin frozen layer had already formed over the hole they'd made. Sammy's snout had to break through it, and she lifted her head slightly to get away from the cold water as he slid her in too. The arrow followed.

When it was as done as it would be, they drifted home through the dark woods, hoping to wake up. They moved along the roadside, close enough to the tree line to hide from a few slow-passing cars. Their headlights illuminated the fast, stinging snow.

Ambrose shoved his bloody coat underneath the roots of an upturned tree in the woods. He buttoned his flannel shirt all the way up, and Cale pulled the hood of his sweatshirt around the scratches on his neck. Shaking, they scrubbed the blood from their cold pink hands in the rough snow. And when they got home, feeling that everything was over, there was the police car in the driveway, come to take them away forever. They were evil boys, they knew now.

Harvey Gindewin was standing on the front porch with Joan. She wore only a sweater and had her arms wrapped tightly around her.

"Oh God," she said. "They're freezing."

Joan hurried into the house and Harvey came toward them slowly. They stopped walking. Ambrose blurted out, "Sammy ran away." His voice was desperate. This loss, the most immediately accessible. "We went to find her."

Harvey put his knee down at their feet and looked up at them through the falling snow. His forehead crumpled and his eyes shined silver. "Boys," he said, "your father's gone."

II

18

Joan Gindewin had had one child, a daughter named Rose, who was stillborn. But Joan was dreaming of her, warm and light, many years later, when the rattling of the cell phone on her bedside table woke her before dawn. A number she didn't know.

A voice she didn't recognize. "Hi. Harvey's here."

Joan looked over. She was alone. "Who is this?"

"He's in my backyard."

"What?" She sat up, her free hand to her t-shirt collar.

"Sorry, this is Lily Rowe. I got your number from a friend."

"Okay?" It was the first time they'd ever spoken, though they'd exchanged smiles and waves.

"Can you come get him? I don't mean to be rude, but I don't want to call the police either."

"Is he alright?"

"I mean, he's walking around with a flashlight. So, um . . ." Lily paused. "He didn't seem to want any coffee. Is that unusual?"

By the time Joan got there, Harvey had moved on from the Rowes'. He stood down the road, on the edge of the field where his friend had crashed all those years ago. The temperature had dropped in the night, turning the wet snow powdery. The rising sun cast a peach glow all around them, and the road steamed in places where the sunlight hit the pavement. Joan pulled up next to him. Harvey got in the passenger seat, and she drove away without a word. In their driveway, she didn't turn off the car. She kept her hands on the wheel, staring straight ahead. "You gotta stop."

His fingers fumbled in the front pocket of his wool jacket, which was too thin for this weather, she thought. He pulled out a folded index card and handed it to her. It read: "Abe's here."

"This is what you gave her?"

He stared at her, seeming to nod without movement.

"This is what you're doing now?"

He grimaced. He got out and shut the door. She watched him slowly cross through the headlights, her foot still on the brake pedal. She found her hand on the stick.

Harvey retired from the Macoun Police Department in 1994. In his sterling tenure of almost forty years, he'd been known to dive into icy rivers, run into burning homes, and shoot when the shot needed to be taken, which had amounted to a handful of rabid racoons and one coyote. Still, it was understood that he'd do what must be done. He could be counted on when it mattered most. Before the Abe and Ray Rowe missing persons cases, he'd inherited a couple of others, including those of his friend Eli's mother, Mary Casey, as well as another woman in town. But the previous sheriff had gathered very little information on those earlier ones, and in the old days, Harvey knew, people could just pick up and leave. Start over anew somewhere else, if they wanted, without being obliged to say goodbye. For the most part, Joan understood, Harvey believed his primary purpose was to be a peacekeeper. To protect people's freedom, safety, and property, and otherwise mind his own business.

A year into retirement, Harvey said he was bored and wasn't earning when he felt he could've been. He went back to work as the head of security at an insurance company's headquarters. In his absence, the Macoun Police Department grew. When he'd started, he was the only officer. And now, they had six. It seemed excessive to Harvey, but it had been after his time that local kids began riding Oxy to robbery and the Horse. The prescription opioids came up the little artery of Route 44, right through town, and in time the heroin followed it north. Nothing new anywhere. Junkies in the woods, same as in the streets.

After his second retirement, this time from the insurance company, Harvey planned to write a book for the historical society, in honor of the town's approaching sestercentennial, its 250-year anniversary. His idea was to dedicate it to his daughter, Rose, who'd been born and never drawn a breath, fifty years before, on the day of the town's bicentennial celebration.

He and Joan couldn't bear to stay in the hospital and they had come back that day to the hoopla, red and blue ribbons wrapping the three wooden light poles on the town green. They heard a fife and drum band. A small crowd waved as they passed, some folks craning their necks to get a glimpse of the new baby that wasn't with them. When Joan had gone into labor the day before, there'd been plenty of chat about the prospect of a momentous shared birthday. Their child was destined, people said, to be king or queen of Macoun.

Later, for the book, Joan helped Harvey set up his study. She got him banker's boxes to store his notebooks for rough drafts and to organize his research, some of which included case notes from his days as a cop. She surprised him with his first laptop and a printer. He feigned enthusiasm. She also got him a good ergonomic chair with lumbar support. He'd built a desk for this new chapter of his life, and Joan positioned it in the center of the room, with a good view out the window to the gardens, where she'd be working.

Joan's sister Catherine, who lived in North Carolina near her three daughters and their kids, gave Joan her first rosebush in 1973, on what was or would've been Rose's first birthday. It led eventually to the planting of dozens of varieties. In time, people from all over the area began making detours to drive by the Gindewins' to see the roses in June. In Bellewood and Nevin and Danvy and even farther away, people who didn't know the Gindewins by name knew the rose house. In the beginning, Harvey felt it was too conspicuous and incongruous with his role. The chief of police living in a floral attraction, a reminder of their secret pain for all to see. But caring for the rose gardens, nurturing each thorny plant, brought Joan some peace, and that was enough for him.

Harvey's stroke came a few weeks into his second retirement, permanently pausing his book, it seemed. This new tragedy fit, in a way, Joan felt. She'd envisioned a period of reflection and leisure, but so quickly that just went right out the window, she once told Kate Casey.

Joan went into Harvey's study the morning she was awakened by Lily Rowe's call, which was Thursday, March 10, 2022. Harvey spent several hours in that room each day. She respected his privacy and presumed he was trying his hardest to continue working on the book, on his tribute to their daughter. What she found was that the materials he'd been reviewing were about Eli Casey's accident. She flipped through the papers on his desk.

The state police had concluded that the accident was just that. An accident. A fluke thing. They happen every day, Joan thought, somewhere else. Though Harvey had little evidence to the contrary, he'd long felt that it just didn't add up. And for years, he couldn't let it go. The man he was after, Abe Rowe, had skipped town, Joan knew, around that time, presumably with his troubled son.

Joan understood that Harvey and Eli were friends. In fact, she'd met her husband through Eli. But she thought he'd finally put that case to rest, and it hurt her to find out that this was what he was really up to. That during this time that she thought was dedicated to their daughter, he was in fact thinking about someone else. A friend, yes, but not their blood. Joan opened the closet to put away some of the boxes.

"He never forgave himself for what happened to those kids," Joan said, when Kate Casey stopped by later that afternoon. But Kate didn't ask which kids. She'd come to ask if she'd left Sadie's blanket there after her session with Harvey. Her arrival startled Joan, who'd been staring at the bare canes of a bush in the front yard, ruminating.

Joan said, "Not sorting out that mess was the only blemish in what was a good career, I suppose." She shook her head. "Not that there was any solving it. But I guess it's obvious now that he never stopped blaming himself, right?"

"Why would he do that?" Kate asked, distracted, something else visibly on her mind. She wore a gray t-shirt taut over her belly and a long cardigan. Her face looked pale and pained. The window of her minivan was lowered a few inches so she could see the top of Sadie's head. She was playing with some plastic dinosaurs in her car seat. The blanket was not found. It wasn't there.

"I think he thinks he waited too long to do something," Joan said. "People have said that. People who don't know any better about how things actually work. Terry Silbey, for one. He said it about twenty years ago when we went into the Fish House bar, and we haven't been back since. Harvey refuses."

"What's he care what that fool says?"

"He doesn't, generally. But I think he thinks he was right. Something just never quite made sense about it. The old 'what could've been.'"

"If only."

"Exactly."

"Yeah," Kate said, turning toward the road as a town truck passed, the plow blade scraping. "So, how well do you know this Lily Rowe?"

"Not much, and plenty," Joan said, eyeing her, not mentioning for the moment the phone call that morning. It wasn't lost on her that some people said she ought to put Harvey in a nursing home, but she didn't want that for either of them. She understood there was a danger in going on the way they were, but when wasn't there danger?

"Like what?" Kate asked.

"I've known of her since they came to town," she said. "And maybe that's what I mean. Harvey said right away they were bad news, the father, anyway, and the son. But you can't just go arresting someone because you don't like them. Because you believe they're no good. Getting the facts, the history, proof. Things moved slower then."

"They still do sometimes."

"Except when they don't." Joan laughed, expecting some repartee from Kate, who didn't smile. The darkness of her mood became clear.

Kate asked, "Do you know if her and Am ever . . . ?"

Joan nodded. "I see."

"He's been acting a little off, I guess."

"Work stress maybe?"

"Yeah. And sometimes this is a hard time of year for him."

"Hm."

"I don't know," Kate said. "Something just feels different."

Joan squeezed her shoulder. "She's got nothing on you, babe."

"I'm a fucking whale," Kate whispered, eyes on Sadie. "I feel like shit all the time."

"I'm sorry," Joan said. "Soon enough. And you look like a million bucks to me."

"Thanks, but spare me."

"I'll let you know if that blanket turns up."

"Right." Kate started moving toward the van.

"Oh, wait. Hang on." Joan hurried into the house. Kate went over to Sadie, who kept mashing the dinosaurs together, making sounds of explosions. Joan came out carrying a tan jacket on a coat hanger. It was ragged, but clean. "Found this in the closet in Harvey's study."

"Okay?"

She handed it over. "Look at the tag." Written in a faded silver metallic marker was the name A. CASEY.

"How old is this?"

"I have no idea," Joan said. "He must've left it here who knows when. Looks like the moths had a field day, but maybe one day when your new little guy is bigger, he'll wear it, like his daddy."

"Maybe," Kate said, taking the jacket. "Maybe on some Halloween."

"There you go. Thought it could be worth a laugh, and then a decent rag, anyway."

19

Lily couldn't focus at work the morning Harvey Gindewin appeared in her backyard. She watched some electricians running wires into a raceway with no sense of why they were doing it, though she'd explained how she wanted it done the day before. Harvey had spooked her. No visitors for decades, and then in one week, two different men coming around the house in the dark. And then the knowing yet absent look in the old man's eyes. His silence. The note.

She wondered what he knew. Because he was right about one thing: Abe was there. She'd reburied his body in the back corner of her property when she was nineteen, as soon as the house was hers. She moved it from the place in the woods where she and Ray had hidden it first.

"We need the feeders," someone said. An electrician in a hard hat and neon-yellow vest stood beside her. "For the panelboard. We're short one."

"What do you want me to do about it?"

"Nothing, I'm just telling you. I'll be right back."

"You didn't inventory right."

"No, we just missed one."

"You're always missing one," she said. "You damn fool."

He looked confused. "It'll take me ten minutes."

She stepped back like she might take a swing at him. "Quit slowing us down."

"I'll be fast. Sorry." With a mystified expression and a cower, he hurried off. She'd never taken a sick day, but it seemed like today might be the day for it.

Her phone buzzed and she expected another new problem. She hesitated, but answered. It was Joe Wheeler. He said he'd gone over to Gibbs Pond to get ready for the dredge and found Ambrose Casey there. Joe's voice was tense. "He said there'd been a change of plans and you'd hired him instead to do it?"

"That's not true," she said.

"Really?" he said. "Wow. This guy."

"He's still there?"

"He better hope not."

"Don't do anything, Joe. Don't worry about it. The job's yours."

"It's like he's trying to take money right out of my hand." As he spoke, his voice got louder, angrier, like he was working himself up into action.

"Joe."

"I got a family too. I known this guy most my life. He says he's my friend. And he just makes up, what? Like I'm just gonna roll over?"

"Joe."

"My youngest, she's gotta get her tonsils out, adenoids. Tubes in her ears, probably."

"Joe. Listen."

"Poor kid. You think that's cheap? He probably knows that too."

"Joe, shut the fuck up! Shut up. Stop talking, okay? Shut up."

He shut up.

"Don't do anything," she said.

"Like hell."

"You want the job?"

"What do you want me to say?"

"Say that you're getting out of there. I'm on my way. I'll straighten it out."

"Yeah." He hung up.

Lily reached the Gibbs place right as Joe was pulling out of the driveway. She slowed to turn in. Through his car window, she saw his nose was bleeding. The bald dome of his head appeared to shine, and she couldn't immediately understand why he suddenly looked so different to her. Then she realized she'd never seen him without a hat before. He peeled out, his tires kicking loose gravel.

Ambrose was standing in the driveway, holding an old baseball cap.

"What'd you do?" she shouted through her open window before she'd even parked.

"He forgot his decoration." Ambrose shrugged, feigning innocence. He held up the baseball cap.

"He was bleeding."

"I barely tapped him."

"You beat the shit out of him?"

"I wouldn't say that," he said. He shook his head and looked at her with concern. "Who knew Joe could be so rude?"

"You think this is funny?"

"No." He dropped the act.

"What is going on with you?"

"I want the job." He walked up and stood beside her window.

"You've made that clear." She opened the door and bumped him back with it. "Now that's a tap. You bleeding?"

"I need the job."

She got out and stared at him. He was well over six feet and had more than a foot on her. They were so close that she had to tilt her head back to see into his eyes. She quickly looked away. "Is your business in trouble?"

"Yes." He went and sat on his truck's bumper.

"That's why you offered to do it for free?"

"Well." He rubbed his jaw. "I was thinking you'd try before you buy, and then you'd buy, buy, buy?"

"I'm about to have two major developments start, and we're gonna be shorthanded. You're missing the forest through the trees here."

He looked at her earnestly, but his eyes shifted. "I'll just tell you the truth," he said. "It's more than the job, and wanting it done right. I love this place. I've wanted to buy it my whole life. I always planned on it. Last time I fished with my dad was here, so there's that."

Conjuring his father caught her off guard, though his father was why she'd come to him in the first place. She owed a debt she could not repay, but she felt a little something was better than nothing. She crossed her arms. "You want it for your own?"

"Correct. For my family."

"What does your wife think about that?"

"She's amenable to it, I think," he said.

"Not very convincing."

"It'll take some convincing, yes. You think Gerlano would sell it, if I got the money right?"

"He loves money, but no. He's been playing a long con on this property for years. Now he's betting big on a post-Covid suburban resurgence and he's just going to be buying up Macoun, in particular, because it's cheap."

"I'm going to talk to him," he said.

"I wouldn't bother." She shook her head. "Because it's done. Let it go. It's not gonna be what it was ever again. So move on."

"We'll see," he said.

"What's to see?"

He stood. "You think Joe's the type to press charges?"

"I'll ask him when he starts the work here."

He came over to her and handed her Joe's hat. "With my best wishes."

She took it by the brim with reticence and a faint disgust, as if it were an old banana peel he'd asked her to throw away.

"I'm going to talk to my brother about that money."

"You're not the best listener, are you?"

"Sometimes, no."

She looked at the hat. "How's he doing, anyway?"

He turned away. "Don't know. Heard he's rich now, though." He didn't look at her again, she noticed, as he got into his truck and pulled out onto the road. The sun had dropped behind the hills. A robin flew from a leafless viburnum in front of the old house. The annual return of that bird used to signal spring there, but they'd stopped migrating. Now they just stayed through winter, shivering. Lily wondered if they'd gotten tougher or stupider, or if the world had just gotten too unpredictable to warrant a trip with no guarantees. Had the birds become resigned?

With Ambrose gone, she started down the old dirt two-track to the water. She'd gone there as a kid, as a teenager, out walking, looking for Ray, thinking. But she hadn't considered that she'd feel some nostalgia for that place. That wasn't her way, she thought. To her surprise, though, she began questioning why they should develop it at all. A nice place like the one Gerlano had in mind would boost her property value, but she'd never sell anyway. Not unless Ray came back to help with the bones.

She couldn't bear to do that alone again. She felt too old, and it'd been too hard.

She came down the hill to the pool and looked up at the crags and ledges. Her brother had found comfort and safety in the cave there, she knew. He'd been drawn to that land, same as Ambrose. Same probably as Ambrose's father, who'd come by her house all those years before, trying to help. And look what it got him.

20

Ambrose had learned of Cale's financial success through their mother. She'd left Macoun for the Connecticut shore as soon as her second son started college. Years later, she got married again, this time to an insurance man, name of Dan, and they moved to a New Hampshire lake, where their life became breeding and raising German shorthaired pointers. Cale skipped the wedding, a muted affair, a small ceremony, a lunch. Her disappointment at his absence was tempered with relief, Ambrose knew. His brother had been a problem for a long time by then. Sensitive and volatile and drunk. He said he only lost it when he came home. So he didn't come home, even though the wedding was on the shore, on the Sound, an hour south of Macoun. A place plenty different in its contours, it was still too close for him.

At his jobsite, Ambrose tried calling his brother again from the seat of a skid steer. He wasn't going to ask for help, other than a loan on a down payment, maybe a cosigner.

Once again, he didn't leave a voicemail, wary of leaving an incriminating clue. You couldn't turn on the TV without seeing some court case where they pulled phone records, lawyers reading people's emails aloud. Everything was forever now, and none of it mattered, he felt, until it did. Until they brought your past back to you and you had to stand trial for what you were.

The advancements in forensic technology also concerned him. Ancient cold cases reopened and closed with a single strand of hair. What could still be on that body, after so much time submerged? He couldn't know. Despite his wariness of the new tech, there he was flopping around conspicuously in plain sight. Showing up at Lily Rowe's, punching Joe Wheeler, talking too much, he knew. He felt the pressure and the desperation squeezing his head from the inside, tightening his neck, popping in his ears. It was all happening so fast, and he had no control over an unfolding that had the power once more to rip apart his family.

He cursed himself for waiting. All this time, he'd resented Cale's seeming freedom. He'd run away. He hadn't been able to deal with it, hadn't been strong enough. And Ambrose felt he'd been stuck, forced to stay behind and protect it. But what had he really done? Sure, he worked, went back to school eventually, studied his trade, dated a lot of women, started a family, launched a business. But he'd avoided this critical problem, out of fear, which had led to helplessness. For all his fighting and the old tough talk, he'd been too afraid, he saw now, to do what he always knew he must. His sense of being a protector, a guardian, was false. He should've left also, and now it was too late.

He parked in front of the town hall. He'd had vague notions of talking to Terry Silbey, who was on the zoning and land use board. He wanted to verify that what Lily had said was true. But in the process, he worried, he could tie himself with another thread to whatever might be found. Did he really think he was going to uncover the bit of red tape that could tangle up Gerlano and his lawyers enough to stop them? After so many years, he still didn't have a plan. Didn't have a clue what to do.

He checked the clock in the dash. It was almost five, and it occurred to him that Terry was probably two vodkas deep already at the Fish House bar. That would be an easier and more natural setting to talk to him anyway, he felt. More coincidental. On the drive over, he called Kate to tell her he had to work late again and wouldn't be home in time for dinner or Sadie's bedtime routine for the third night in a row.

"Is everything okay with you?" she asked.

"Yeah, sure," he said.

"What's going on, Am?"

"Just a little snafu with the job. This doctor's a real pain."

She didn't sound convinced, and when he hung up, he wondered if that was the first time he'd lied to his wife. Then he remembered that, no, he'd lied the other nights he came home late too. And actually, he'd lied all along.

He wasn't the man she thought she'd married, and never had been.

Ambrose didn't see Terry Silbey at the Fish House. Three women, teachers he recognized from Kate's work functions, sat at one of the small square tables against the wall. He avoided their eyes. He didn't know any of the others at the bar in that dim space. Guys in canvas work jackets and faded hoodies beneath the Christmas lights, under the décor of nets and old rope, the same old wicker chandelier. The bartender, Alice, had worked there as long as Ambrose could remember and looked it. She'd seen Bonnie Rowe dancing on tables, taking off her sweatshirt to rapt attention. Later, she'd served Ambrose beers when he was in high school. Gravelly voice, pack of Kools by the register. He ordered a pilsner and sat at the bar in a corner with his back to the wall.

Setting the beer bottle on a coaster, she said, "Been a while. How you?"

"Thirsty. You?"

"Always. How come we don't see you no more?"

"Family."

"Is that good or bad?" She laughed, a rattling cackle.

He nodded. "Good."

She stopped laughing immediately, as if her off switch had been thrown.

"You seen Terry Silbey?" he asked.

"He's gone sober again," she said. "Try back next week." She laughed again, and the sound of it made him itch, jangled like broken metal in his ears. Jimmy Buffett played through the tinny overhead speakers. "Why Don't We Get Drunk and Screw?" was the song. Alice turned her attention to a big man at the end of the bar who'd come in and begun pressing on a stool top.

"This one good?" he asked.

"Should be," she said. "But go easy on this one, Lenny."

Ambrose knew Lenny Denard, though they'd never spoken. When Lenny looked over, Ambrose raised his beer.

He nodded. Ordered a Baileys Irish Cream and whiskey and fish and chips. After, Lenny said, "What are you doing for work these days?"

"Homebuilder."

"You take over your dad's company?"

"He was better at it."

"Good builder."

"You?"

"Crane operator." He tilted his head and raised his eyebrows, a look that suggested he was waiting for Ambrose to ask where, but Ambrose knew already that he worked for Gerlano too. Maybe they all would, soon enough.

"Good talking to you." Ambrose left. He passed the Gibbs place again on his way home and slowed when he saw a car in the driveway, facing the road, headlights off. Its interior electronics cast a faint blue glow. The car was positioned the way a cop might run a speed trap, but it was an older SUV, a Bronco, it looked like, not one of the Ford Explorers the town cops drove now. He wondered if it was an undercover, or a Hartford drug dealer come to make a drop in the sticks. In all the times he'd passed that house, at least twice a day his whole life, he'd never seen someone staked out like that, and it added to the mounting pressure, the ticking in his head.

When he got home, the house was dark. It was only a little after seven. Kate was in bed, he knew, but he didn't go into their downstairs bedroom. He went to the kitchen and pulled another beer from the fridge. He sat at the table and saw himself reflected again amid all the objects of his domestic life, the only home he'd ever known. Then he stared through the glass into the darkness beyond. He needed to act fast. He needed to have acted fast already. He needed to let that go so he could act now. But any wisp of a plan that popped into his head continued to blow away. He felt he needed to do it all alone, but he knew, too, that he couldn't.

The floorboards creaked in the living room and he turned to see Kate sway into the dim hallway toward him.

"What are you doing?" she said.

"Nothing." He turned to the wall.

She paused in the doorway and studied him. "Are you crying?"

"No." He sniffled.

Her face crumpled. "Am, please. Tell me."

He looked at her as she approached him. The only light on was the bulb above the sink, across the room.

"Are you seeing someone else?" she said.

"Never," he said.

But she could see it was bad and she stiffened beside him, bracing herself. "Is it that Lily Rowe?"

He shook his head.

"What is it?" She put her hand on the back of his neck.

He bowed his head forward, hands in his lap. "I've told you everything," he said. "Except one thing."

21

The airplane shimmied in the dark, bouncing over the Pacific, and the pill bottle shook in Cale's hand. The old tablets had turned to powder and clotted up in the bottle. He hadn't needed them in years, and now he had too much anxiety about taking the antianxiety medication to take it anyway. But he held the bottle like a talisman, slick in his hand. He closed his eyes. He could feel the woman in the seat across the aisle watching him.

Kate had called his office that Thursday afternoon around three o'clock, Hawaii time. She called again ten minutes later, and again five minutes after that. She said it was a family emergency. And when the receptionist came into his office and suggested that the caller was very upset and that maybe he should take the call, he relented, so she wouldn't say he hadn't. Some new bad news, he thought, regarding his mom, Ambrose, maybe the little girl. He'd never spoken to Kate before, though the emails she'd sent him had been friendly. So she surprised him with a commanding tone: "It's time to come home."

He said, "I am home?"

"Am told me."

"Told you what?"

"You know what." She waited.

"What is this?"

"They're digging it up. Early next week. There's no time. You have to get on the next flight."

"I don't know what you're talking about," he said, feeling choked.

"Yes, you do. He stayed to protect it. You ran away. But now you have to come back and deal with it. He can't do it alone, and there's no one else."

"I have no interest in this."

"No one does."

"I have to go."

"Listen," she said, keeping him from hanging up. "I'm not losing my family because you've been a coward for too long. You'll lose everything too. Your career, your money, your freedom. Everything. We all will. Do you understand that?"

"This is my work line." He grew suddenly angry.

"Maybe not for long."

"You can't call here like this." He became indignant. "Talk to me here like this."

"Whatever you've got going on out there, Reese. Right, you're Reese? Well, kiss it goodbye if you don't come now. Because if you don't, and if it goes the way no one wants it to, I'll be sure they know who did what."

"Are you threatening me?"

"See you tomorrow, brother." She hung up.

Cale locked his office door and paced. In a way, he'd been expecting this news since his brother started calling, since the return of the nightmares, and before that too, since the beginning of it all. He was terrified, but he knew. The time had come. And considering the prospect of a sudden return, of it all coming to light at last, to his surprise he felt a tinge of relief, however faint. He sat down and booked his flight for that evening, without any due diligence. He realized later that that was a credit to Kate, who'd convinced him of this urgency so thoroughly that he believed it immediately to be the truth. He left the office, telling the receptionist his brother was sick and he needed to go.

"Family first," she said. "You're a good brother."

"No, I'm not." He didn't stop or look back.

In the air, in his aisle seat, he was exhausted, but his nightmares had made him fearful of sleep again. Still, he nodded off into that space between waking states, coming to every time his chin dropped to his chest. He was thankful that he dreamt of nothing. The plane descended toward Bradley Airport a little before one in the afternoon on Friday. Through the window, he saw the treed hills and the Connecticut River. He felt worn thin after so much travel, a half day in the air, a six-hour leap forward in time, and seven well-spaced vodkas that failed to knock him out efficiently enough. He got a rental car and changed into one of the three suits he'd brought in his garment bag.

After a late lunch of cashews, he called Gerlano's office from the road. His intention, despite wavering confidence, was to project success. He willed an assured smile that he felt would come through in his voice. Gerlano's executive assistant answered, sounding harried. Cale explained that his name was Reese, and he was a real estate investor with an exciting proposal. All parties, he explained, would benefit from a meeting this afternoon.

She told him no. Gerlano's schedule was completely booked solid for three weeks.

"Great," he said. "I'll be right over."

"I don't think you heard what I said."

"I really appreciate you both accommodating me on such short notice," he said.

"Sir?"

"Remind me your name again?" he said.

"Marcia. And who are you?"

"Marcia, you really are the best. I look forward to seeing you in fifteen minutes. Can I bring you anything? It's no trouble."

"Do not come here. Security won't let you in."

"Great, talk soon. Bye now."

Doing his best Reese, he felt new again in a place that was old to him. He knew Nevin well. When he was a kid, it felt like a big town. He thought, for a moment, that he was returning as a winner near the place where he'd turned into a loser. And it was less likely someone would recognize him in Nevin so many years later. So he could act. He could pretend. That had worked. Learning that had cost a lot.

With a knowing smile and his cell phone to his ear, he went past the security desk, where a sleepy-looking guard with a crew cut glanced up from his own phone. "Wait," he managed, but Cale was halfway up the stairs already, telling his phone, "I'm coming up the stairs right now, Mister Gerlano. Sorry for the delay." He went straight to the corner office, greeting Marcia as if they'd met many times before. "I forgot if you were more a flowers or a chocolate person." He smiled. "So, I brought neither. Next time, I promise."

She stood as he went into the office, following a quick two-tap knock. She said, "What are you doing? I'm calling security."

Seated at his desk now, Gerlano looked up from his work.

"I've come to make you an even richer man," Cale said.

"No solicitors."

"Sorry to disturb you, sir. I know you're busy, so I'll get right to the point. My name is C. Reese Casey." He reached into his interior jacket pocket for his business card. "And I'm not selling. I'm interested in buying a piece of property you're currently holding." Cale extended his business card across the desk, holding it between his index and middle finger.

Gerlano didn't take it. "Which?"

He continued to hold out the business card. "Here's my card."

It remained untaken. "Which property?"

"Six thirty-two Apple Brook Road."

"No."

"Whatever you're paying, I'll double it." He put the card down on the desk.

Gerlano stood and picked up a golf putter that was resting against the wall behind him. "And when I'm done with it, it'll be worth ten times that."

"Maybe. And maybe not. That doesn't account for your cost to get it there, and we both know you'll be doing that work and launching the property in a recession."

"What do you think I am, some nickel-and-dimer? You think I'm just going to abandon something I've worked on for years when some slick unvetted hack pops into my office to interrupt me unannounced?"

"You're right," Cale said. "That is fair. I did call ahead, though."

"Get out of here." He rested the putter on his shoulder.

Cale nodded. "Maybe I didn't make myself clear?"

"Get out of here right now."

"If I were a seller in your position, I'd react the same way you are."

He took the putter off his shoulder and squeezed the grip with both hands like it was a baseball bat. "I don't give a shit what you think."

Cale stared at him. "You're gonna do something with that little putter, are you, big guy?"

"I got a Glock in my drawer too. And on my property, I'll stand my ground."

"Look, let's just reset, okay?" Cale said. "I get it. No one wants someone showing up in their office end of day Friday, when they're trying to wrap for the week."

"Get the fuck out," he screamed, his face red, the cords of his neck straining. "Marcia, call security. Call the cops."

"Yes, sir, right away," she called into the office. "For the record, I did not sanction this meeting."

"I understand you're stressed," Cale said. "I would be too, if I were stuck carrying a giant piece of land that is ultimately undevelopable, given the many precious migratory species that call that wetlands habitat home."

"You think we haven't talked to Wetlands?"

"Locally, sure. But the state, the federal government? They're not this fast."

"This isn't my first rodeo, you clown."

"Nor is it mine. Thanks for your time and consideration." He bid Gerlano adieu and briskly headed for the emergency exit. The alarm didn't sound when he hit the door. Keeping his head down, he hustled to his rental car. Distracted for a moment, he saw a woman getting out of a black pickup. She wore work boots and jeans, and she had a beauty, he felt, that shined like obsidian, smooth and dark and sharp enough to cut. He didn't recognize her at first, until she squinted at him and said, "Cale?"

22

Joan Gindewin found out about Meryl Gibbs from Joe Wheeler's wife, Laura, whom she ran into at the pharmacy. Joan was mystified by the double news of the death and the sale of her neighbor's land. "She passed on months ago and no one told us?"

"The obit was in the *Courant* yesterday." Laura was small and large-toothed, her hair a rusty hue. Her nickname growing up had been Chip, for Chipmunk. Joan knew that Laura had hated being named after a rodent until high school, when she embraced it as something that made her unique and memorable. And that's when everyone just started calling her Laura.

"Who runs an obit so long after?" Joan asked. "There was no funeral?"

"Maybe in Florida?"

"It's not right."

"Only person mentioned left behind was her son,

Rodney," Laura said. "So that's who she had left. That's where she was at."

"She was born here and lived here almost all her life."

"Eighty-eight, not too shabby." Laura shrugged, switching hands with the store's red plastic shopping basket. In it, she had two boxed ice packs and Band-Aids half covering a tube, Joan noticed, of Preparation H. "Did Lily Rowe ever reach out to you?"

Joan pretended she didn't hear the question. "Just selling her place before she's even had a decent send-off?"

"She texted me for your number really early the other day. I still had it from the children's fair bake sale."

Joan leaned against a shelf stocked with paper towels. "Doing it like that before people could pay their respects. Lord, the priorities. It's sickening to think of it. The son. Is nothing sacred? I mean, the Gibbses lived there going back all the way, before the town was even incorporated, since the beginning. Is this the way it's going be now?"

"Joe said her son always seemed like an odd duck," Laura said.

"I'd call this a case in point, to the extreme."

"Well, sometimes people just need the money."

"I know it." Joan nodded.

"He looked like a pedophile, people said. The son."

Joan's expression betrayed her confusion. "What?"

"In his sixties, unmarried. Mustache, they say. A weird one. One of those slimy little skinny ones. The mustache." Laura lifted a jar of peanuts from the shelf and appeared to read the listed ingredients. "Season pass to Disney, I heard. Must be nice. Some people, right?"

"What's it you're saying now?" Joan asked.

"Tell you what, I'm excited for it. I heard there'll be a nice little restaurant and things like that, hot tubs."

"How'd you hear?"

"Joe got it from Lily Rowe," she said. "He's gonna clear out the brook there for them. Though maybe I'm not supposed to say that? It's all been Murtry's Law, I swear. First, he slips and bonks his face bad, and now his machines seem to all be going wonka-doo."

"We're right downstream." Joan looked toward the door. "They can't just go digging out the waterways. There's a permitting process, at the least."

"Nothing against the general store." Laura put the peanuts back on the shelf. "But imagine somewhere right down the road where you can get a nice dinner, some wine. You and Harvey could walk."

"Where's the public hearings and due process? I haven't heard anything about this fly-by-night business."

"You wouldn't even have to drive." Laura laughed, her face scrunching, cheeks flaring. Her eyes drifted and she seemed to be playing out some imaginary scenario in her mind. "Heck, you could have two glasses of wine. Or a whole bottle, right? Why not? Special occasion."

Joan watched her laugh for a few more seconds before she said, "Alright, then."

"Where are you off to now?"

"Town hall."

Laura stopped laughing. "What're you gonna say?"

"I just want to know the truth," Joan said.

"What's to know? I just told you."

"No, I don't think you did."

Terry Silbey, at the town hall, was light on facts too. He admitted he'd had a call with some people at Valley Development Corp. and, given the size of the proposed project, and the fact that the pool had been dug out and dredged historically by the Gibbses in the ice-farming days, he told them it sounded like they'd only need a general permit. "It doesn't matter anyway," he said. "They called back to say they decided not to do it at all. They're just going to leave it alone for now, until it's all buttoned up."

"The whole thing?"

"No, the dredge. The construction is moving forward, at least the permitting. You seen what they're putting up in Nevin?"

"Unfortunately," Joan said. A piece of plexiglass separated them, a Covid sneeze guard that would never come down now. Terry sat in his swivel chair in what looked like a wood-paneled phone booth. Mostly he just sat there all day doing nothing, watching videos on his phone. People didn't stop in to ask questions like they used to, or require a face-to-face exchange involving pen and paper. When they did, he told them to go check the website. In his job, he'd become mostly a sign directing people to the Internet. A public servant with a pension.

"You kidding?" he said. "It's giving the whole town a face-lift."

"And what kind of face is it?" Joan said. "One of these poor starlets turned into a cat?"

"Oh, come on, Joan. It's not all bad. They'll be selling fancy ice creams and hand creams, and God, everything."

"Don't need it." She crossed her arms. "I'm gonna fight it."

He laughed at her, a big belly laugh from a small fat man with thin limbs and fingers. He was bald on top with bushy gray hair on the sides. He quickly gathered his composure. "You're gonna fight who? Valley?"

"Yeah, Terry. I am. And the town, if I have to, and you. It just doesn't smell right." She looked into her purse. "Mint?"

"Ha." He leaned back in his chair. "And how's Harvey, then?"

"He still doesn't like you, if that's what you mean."

"Could be that's a two-way street, right?" He smoothed one side of his short mustache with a quick flick of his tongue.

She wrinkled her nose involuntarily at the sight. "Everything's a two-way street, at least when you're driving home from the Fish House, isn't it?"

He nodded, chewing the inside of his cheek. "Never much happening in this town, nothing for the cops to do but sit on their thumbs, and pull people over for no reason."

"Yeah, no reason. Dragging someone's fence."

"And then, when there's real bad guys like that Abe Rowe, beating his kids, doing you-know-what in the dump swap shack, really swerving around, and what? Don't have time to take care of that. Outfoxed. He's in the wind. Isn't that something. A real hero when there's a big bad squirrel broken into someone's screen porch, but a real threat to this town . . . ?"

She stared him, and then forced a smile. "Glad you got your license back again. I thought they background-checked you to work here. Your daddy still has pull then, does he? Good for him."

"Thanks, I heard he can't talk now. Harvey. That's too bad."

"And too bad you still can."

Joan fumed on the ride home, sharper insults coming to her. Terry Silbey, the town fool, she thought, and yet in a position of power, however limited. Wasn't that just how it was. She was wondering what she could do to oust him as she pulled into her driveway to find Kate Casey watching Sadie run across the lawn, threatening to tip over at every turn.

Kate waved to Joan. "Sick of me yet?"

"Never," Joan said. "I'd say it was a lucky week, if I didn't just talk to the two most annoying people in town." In the pause, where Kate might've asked her to name them or elaborate, she didn't. Joan got out of the car and put her hands on her knees, giving Sadie a big wide-eyed smile. "Hey, Sadie baby. You running?" Joan swooped her up in her arms. "Wow, you're getting so fast, aren't you?"

"I'm fast," Sadie said. "I'm running."

"Sadie wanted to see your roses."

"Nothing to see yet. But is that true, Sadie? You want to take a look?"

Kate said, "I just read some research about a new technique for regaining language for people with aphasia."

"Okay," Joan said, bringing Sadie to the nearest bush.

"Is Harvey here?"

"He takes a nap around now, usually." Joan pointed to one of the bare canes. "That's called a thorn."

"Forn," Sadie said.

"Very good," Joan said. "Ouch."

"Part of the research, the technique, you compare their writing, the letters, before and after," Kate said. "Do you have those cards he's been working on?"

"Sure," Joan said.

"You keep them in his study?"

"Some," Joan said. "Some I threw out. Some are in a drawer."

"You mind if I take a quick look?"

"Be my guest," Joan said, and when Kate went inside, she showed Sadie the first rosebush they planted, the one from her sister, big and largely unpruned compared to the other bushes. "You like it?"

"Yeah," Sadie said. "It's prickers."

Joan smiled, though her face tightened. She shifted Sadie to her right side. Through the window, she saw Kate in the study, picking through one of the banker's boxes.

She held Sadie a little tighter. "This rose, baby, is called Rose."

She thought about how it was Harvey who'd done that planting. She'd spent the bulk of the year in bed. She'd blamed herself for what had happened, because there'd been no one else to blame. The weight of her sadness had been too much.

That June, Harvey made her an invitation, had it professionally done by a printer in Bellewood. Beautiful heavy card stock, embossed lettering. It cordially invited one Mrs. Joan Jane Grey Gindewin to the unveiling of something spectacular. Begrudgingly, she came outside in her robe. He handed her a glass of champagne and pulled off a gold satin sheet he'd used to hide the plant. It looked pathetic, a thin little shrub. But something happened when Joan saw it after so much pomp and circumstance. Something that hadn't happened in a long time. She laughed. It was ridiculous, the whole thing was ridiculous. It was out of character for Harvey, she thought, but he'd surprised her and gone to such great lengths to reach her, she understood. To bring her back into the world.

Through the window she saw Kate Casey leave her husband's study, and she knew then what she had to do. She had to help Harvey. Whatever he was doing with the old case notes and the night walking, she had to stop resisting him and help him find the answers he still sought. She had to help him find that peace.

23

Lily waited for takeout at the bar in her favorite restaurant, a modern Italian American place in Nevin. They made pizza and charred vegetables in a wood oven, so there was firelight, warmth, and bustle. Chefs calling out for ingredients, plates. She could sit there by herself and be left alone, unbothered, watching them work. She smelled the smoke and the dough crisping as she sipped her ice water with lemon. Faded brick walls and dark wood everywhere. Candles burning in stout glass jars, European soccer highlights on a small TV in the corner.

Six stools at the bar, and Lily was at one end. A couple spoke quietly, heads close, at the other. It looked to her as if they felt they had a little invisible blanket draped over them. She wondered if she was jealous, and the answer was mostly no. She understood that she was supposed to want something that looked like that, some kind of closeness with another. She'd tried once to watch a popular television show, in the reality style shaped by producers and editors and executives to show an impossible romantic fantasy used to sell cars and promote tampon brands. She'd liked one episode well enough, but had never tuned in again. It was all too phony.

One of the perks, she found, of being in her forties versus her twenties or even her thirties was that people had begun to intrude less upon her solitude. It made her look forward to her fifties and sixties. She knew the physical pain increased, along with certain difficulties, but she was no stranger to pain. That seemed preferable to staving off inadequate men and unhappy hens trying to set her up on dates with their degenerate kin, or intimating that they were better off than she was because they had a big dumb fatso at home to stink up the bathroom and mow the lawn.

As she watched a cook box up her broccolini with garlic confit and fresh thyme, a woman came and sat in the middle seat. She had short gray hair and wore a black track suit and expensive basketball sneakers.

"Hey, can I buy you a drink?" the woman asked her.

Lily had never once had a sip of alcohol. Her parents had unintentionally made sure of that. "Me?"

The woman nodded again. "Lily, right?"

"How'd you know?"

"I work for Gerlano too," she said.

"Oh? In what capacity?"

"I'm Kit Donohue." She swiveled in her seat toward Lily, her legs splayed. She had sharp blue eyes and a thin severe face. Her nose was small, beaked. The overall effect, Lily felt, was that she was talking to a bird of prey dressed for a pickup game at the YWCA.

"The investigator?" Lily said.

Kit nodded and turned back to the bar. "Big project coming up, huh?"

"They're all big projects."

"But this one is right in your backyard, isn't it?" Kit stared at her now.

"I wouldn't say it's my backyard."

"Pretty close, though, right?"

A waiter brought Lily's pizza and the broccolini in a plastic to-go bag and left it on the bar beside her, with a nod.

"Yes and no." Lily grabbed the bag and stood. "Bye."

"I'll be seeing you."

"Maybe. Maybe not."

Lily ate her pizza on the road, driving to the Gibbs property. She tried to parse out her encounter with Kit, whose name she'd heard in the context of due diligence and investigative thoroughness. She remained confused by Kit's presence and angle, and especially her use of the phrase "in your backyard." What could Gerlano know, she wondered. It didn't benefit him financially or otherwise to rattle her about a job that he wanted her to do, but he was an asshole who liked to play games. Then again, there weren't that many restaurants around, at least decent ones, and maybe Kit being there and saying that was just another coincidence.

Lily tried to forget the encounter as she waited for Daniel Canfield in the Gibbses' driveway. She and Gerlano had agreed it wouldn't hurt to have some extra eyes on the place until they got the first part of the job done. Between them, the company line was that there'd be no dredge at all. Plead ignorance. Forgiveness over permission, Gerlano said. No need to raise the hackles of the EPA or anybody else. Just a few drags out of the bottom there to see what they were working with for planning purposes while the rest of the paperwork fell into place. It was a timing issue, and that was one of the reasons she knew she needed to replace Joe Wheeler. He wasn't working out. The man was too emotional, emailing and texting with status updates on the smallest issues. His excavator wouldn't start now. She wondered if Ambrose was sabotaging him. But she didn't have time for that or the rest of it, and she needed more discretion now. So, she decided to bring in an out-of-towner, who could just do the work quick and then be gone. It wasn't her problem that Joe had been embarrassed by his altercation with Ambrose, and she hoped that embarrassment would keep him from bringing in the cops or lawyers for now. It wouldn't help any of her timelines if she wound up being questioned or deposed. She understood she had to move even faster to get the job done now. It had taken on a new dimension, she felt. The stakes were higher with the project so close to where she lived. She was shaping the environment of her future.

And yet, she understood her effort to increase focus on work was also because of Cale. She hadn't seen him since they were teenagers. He'd gone away to boarding schools and hadn't been around in years. Last time she saw him, she was working at the general store. He came in, clearly stoned. His eyes barely open, nearly dripping off his face. She said hi. He took one look at her and burst into tears and ran out. It would've been a laughable encounter, preposterous, if she hadn't felt the same way somehow. She went out back, down to Apple Brook, which ran behind the store. She sat on a dead log, crying herself, feeling horrible about what she and Ray had done to him and his family. She'd forgotten, or had never quite noticed, how much Cale had come to look like his father.

In the parking lot at the Valley offices, all these years later, he'd invited her to dinner. When she said she was slammed with work, he suggested drinks. She told him about her late nights and early mornings, so he floated coffee anytime. The conversation came to a conclusion at the sound of a distant siren. He asked for her number, and she said she thought Ambrose had it, though she knew he didn't.

"I'd rather get it from you."

"I'm in a rush," she said, and she hustled into the building and sat alone in an empty conference room with the lights out. She still felt something for him after so long, she found. In her solar plexus, in her chest, she carried the weight and ache. She couldn't tell if it was love or some kind of self-inflicted wound. The longing for something that could never be. Maybe the impossibility of it made it feel more perfect, gave it power, increasing her desire for things to have been different.

Later, at the Gibbs property, she realized that she didn't need to wait for Daniel to come sit in his car all night, for no reason really. Gerlano was still testing his loyalty and brains, or lack thereof. And she realized, too, that she was waiting for someone else to come instead. She sensed somehow that he'd be there that night at the pond that wasn't really a pond at all. She didn't have a word to describe that feeling, and the closest she could come to it was *supernatural*. Not ghosts or demons, but somehow this feeling of fate coming down.

She'd had that same feeling when she was thirteen. Even with her father gone, she didn't like to be at the house. But one morning, she woke up feeling fine, though she understood she needed to stay home sick anyway. She needed to prevent something horrible from happening, though she didn't know what it was. That's why she was home the day Eli Casey missed the bend. She'd fallen asleep on the couch inside, but woke to a commotion on the front steps. Ray had decided to play hooky too. She heard him yelling. Someone else was there. A man's voice. Waking, she was hit with a dread that it was her father returning. Her legs locked and she felt she might faint.

When she came out on the porch, she saw the severed hands, discolored gray and olive, not even real-looking anymore, like dissolving chunks of rubber, movie props in a Ziploc. She saw Ray running toward Mr. Casey, who was jumping into his truck on the side of the road. Ray had backed their father's truck into the driveway for a quick getaway if they needed one, and he gave chase. The tires whirred. Lily ran out across the icy dirt in her threadbare socks. A paper bag of groceries lay on its side, spilling apples. Passing it, she heard the crunch and shatter of what proved to be Mr. Casey's truck hitting the tree. From the mailbox, she saw her father's truck pulled over down the road and her brother standing beside Casey's driver-side window, peering closely into the cab. Even from that distance, she could see Ray was barefoot, standing on the hard snow crust.

"Ray!" she shouted. "Ray!" When he didn't respond, and just kept standing there, peering in, she shouted that she was calling the police. She was afraid another car might come by, and of course, Seb's house was right back in the woods there.

"Come see this," Ray yelled back. "You gotta see this."

She screamed, "I'm calling now." And she ran back inside. She was dialing, pulling the nine around the circle of the rotary phone, when she saw Ray drive past the house again, going up Waquaheag toward Route 21, over the hill in Danvy. That's what upset her most, feeling he was gone, leaving her behind finally, in the end. The dispatcher answered, and heaving, Lily said she'd heard an accident but didn't know any of the details, and soon the ambulance came for Mr. Casey. She cleaned up the spilled groceries. Though she was hungry, she couldn't eat, and she buried them in the backyard. Gagging and crying, she buried her father's hands too.

She was alone that evening when Harvey Gindewin stopped by asking to speak to her father. Ray wasn't back yet, off to Alaska already, she thought. Her mother had woken up that afternoon and gone down to take a look at the accident scene, where she found Seb standing there, shaking his head. He'd been at the store and missed it all. A bewildered conversation led to an invitation for coffee, which turned into a whiskey, Lily learned later.

"The truck's gone." Lily cried to Harvey on the front porch. "I don't think he's coming back this time."

"It's okay." Harvey put his hand on her shoulder. "You did good today, making that call. If you hadn't been home, he never would've had a chance. And don't worry, he's a fighter."

"My dad hated him." She looked at the cracked rail on the porch. "He hated Mister Casey."

"And why's that?"

"Because he was nice to us." She looked up at him. His eyes startled her, but she'd learned how to deal with more frightening men already. "He tried anyway, and look what that got him. We're cursed."

"Where can I find your dad?"

"I don't know." She cried.

"Did Mister Casey talk to him today? Did you see or hear anything?"

"I was asleep." She sniffled. "But I thought I heard my dad tell someone to get the hell out of here, and then I heard the sound of the tires pulling out, and I saw my dad's truck driving off the other way."

"Your brother wasn't in school today either. Was he with your dad?"

"No, he wasn't," she said. "Ray's been camping out, because he's tired of my dad beating on him."

"He's beating him?" Harvey asked.

"You knew that already, didn't you?" Lily shook her head. She'd come to view most cops as clueless. In all the places they'd been, in all the bad situations, the police had never been able to see what was really happening and help them. It's true Ray had coached her to deny everything with the police, Family Services, teachers, anyone who asked what they shouldn't be asking, and she'd learned how to lie well, knowing that if she didn't, the consequences at home would be much worse. Still, part of her wanted someone in a position to do something to see the truth without her having to tell them.

Harvey said, "I asked you both about that before, and you told me no."

"What do you think we're gonna say?"

"I'm sorry," Harvey said. "What about you? You can tell me. Is he abusive to you too? Your father?"

"Not like he is with Ray." She covered her face with her hands. "Ray won't let him."

"He won't?"

"Whatever he's done, there was a reason. And he's not all bad. People don't know that. That he's not all bad. He can be good too."

Now, years later, in front of Meryl Gibbs's house, waiting for Daniel Canfield, or perhaps some vague notion of fate, Lily saw a dot of light in the woods, small and drifting like a distant firefly. She'd come, she realized, to confess it all to the man whom she'd lied to as a child. So easily, so convincingly, she'd thrown a smart cop off the trail, and sent him on a years-long pointless pursuit of her father. And now, she felt she could confess to the one who couldn't speak. The one no one would believe, though she felt that he'd figured it all out now at last. She was an accomplice in the deaths of two fathers.

A car pulled in behind her. In the dark, she tried to tell its make by the shape of the headlights. Confused when it wasn't Daniel's Bronco, she stared at it, shielding her eyes. The car reversed and receded. And when she looked back to the woods, the light was gone.

24

Ambrose stood outside on the deck of his house in the dark with a black duffel bag over his shoulder. Kate leaned against the doorframe, one hand on her belly and the other on her lower back, which he knew was aching.

"It's too dangerous," she said. "It's too much."

"I know."

She winced and touched her side, but quickly dropped her hand.

"You okay?"

"No," she said. "And so what?" Behind her, strewn across the kitchen table, were some of the papers she'd taken from Harvey's office, including a notebook with pages dated 2005. Written in a steady hand, in blue ink, it appeared to be Harvey's attempt, years after the accident, to remember and reconstruct the trouble between the Caseys and the Rowes, to find the missing pieces. He was well into his tenure in security by then, still trying to make sense of it all, apparently. These pages included no reference to Ambrose's jacket, which had been bloodied and stuffed under a tree, left to rot. Judging by the condition of it, they guessed that Harvey had found it years after Ambrose had hidden it. But then, to their bewilderment, he'd cleaned it, or had it cleaned, and hung it in his closet, without returning it or ever mentioning it.

"Maybe he just forgot," Kate said, and that was the best they could do for an explanation. She had left two other notebooks in the study that seemed less relevant. On the first page of the one she took, underlined at the top, was a note about Abe Rowe's truck. It had been found abandoned two weeks after the storm, on an old logging road on state land in Danvy. A public trail crossed the road. It led hikers up into southwestern Massachusetts. Harvey had walked this trail himself, the notes showed, looking for Abe, but he found only the snow covering everything, and later that spring, nothing.

What worried Kate, she told Ambrose, was the existence of electronic records that might corroborate or add to the incriminating evidence these papers suggested. They each studied them alone. Kate first, and then Ambrose, with trepidation. He still wondered about Abe Rowe, whom he knew his father had not liked. But then, almost no one had liked Abe, outside of maybe a couple of guys at the dump, at the bar. The criminally inclined. And here comes Eli Casey with some groceries, a snack, nothing to last. Nothing to warrant a hero's welcome, from one perspective. He comes onto the property, unasked, knowingly unwanted. Brazen, one could say, antagonistic even. Insulting, surely, to Abe, a man who should've provided for his family but clearly would not or could not. Bottom line, he did not.

When the state police conducted their investigation, Ambrose remembered his mother's fury toward a young detective whose face he never saw. One suggested that maybe Ambrose's dad would've been better off just staying away. Obvious, of course, when you know the ending.

"He got what was coming to him, you're saying?" his mother had asked. She was standing at the front door, which was open only a couple of inches. Ambrose sat on the living room sofa behind her, in stiff dress clothes. His head empty. Or rather, too full to process. In shock.

"I'm just wondering why them," the trooper said.

"Why anyone, is that it?"

"That's what I'm trying to figure out," he said. "There's a lot of hungry families."

"Well, some people look out for others, for kids, especially when they've grown up hard themselves." She slammed the door and turned the deadbolt. "You let us know when you have answers," she shouted and crouched down to her knees. But they didn't come back. Instead they went and questioned Seb Bainer about the accident. He lived right near it after all, and he'd cut down that birch pretty quick, albeit with Harvey's okay. They questioned Bonnie Rowe, too, and Lily, and they looked for Abe and Ray. But it seemed pretty straightforward, they concluded, based on EMT reports, scene analysis, and no evidence inside the cab or elsewhere. The best they could do to explain how the crash had occurred was that maybe Eli had been distracted by something, an animal perhaps, or had nodded off, and the momentary lapse in attention had come at the wrong time. A focused man had briefly lost his focus, and that was it.

After his review of Harvey's papers, Ambrose told Kate that he still hoped Abe would turn up somewhere and pay for what he'd done, the way his son had. She was disappointed. She said she hated lying to Joan for what proved to be, in her estimation, nothing. She didn't know exactly what she'd been hoping to find. She just wanted to know the all of it. She couldn't understand, she told Ambrose, how he could have kept it from her for so long. How she could have built the foundation of her family, her life, with a man who would withhold that critical piece of who and why he was. She still loved him, she said, but she felt misled and betrayed. She understood of course that he may never want to tell others. But it'd made her wonder, too, how well he even knew her. Did he think that she couldn't bear it? That she was some flower who would wilt in its darkness? Did they truly know each other at all, she'd asked in their bed the night he told her. Both dressed, on top of the blankets, facing their walls.

"It was never a good time," he said. "It's not something I like to think about."

"But how often do you?"

"A lot," he said. "These days, almost always."

Through the mattress, he felt her body heave and shake. "It's just the hormones," she said, her voice glassy.

"No, it's not," he said.

"No," she said, steeling herself. "But it's too late to turn back now. So, we do what must be done."

He rolled toward her. "We?"

"My God, I can't believe you went through all that all at once," she said. "You were just a kid. A child." And she turned toward him and put her hand on his cheek, and together they wept.

On the deck later, Ambrose shifted the duffle bag slung on his shoulder as he leaned in to kiss his wife. She pulled back slightly, enough to stop him.

"I love you," he said.

"Be safe," she said. "Be careful."

And he went off into the night, into the same field his grandmother had crossed all those years before he was born. The same one he and Cale had crossed when they came out of those woods the day their lives were split in two. He waited by the old crab apple tree that'd been in the middle of that field his whole life. It'd been broken jagged at the top and charred by lightning. The night was cold and the stars clear. The moon was three-quarters full, in the phase called waxing gibbous. He didn't remember where he'd learned that phrase, but it'd struck him with its strangeness and stayed with him. The moonlight on the crust of snow gave his dim world an eerie paleness. He could see patches of dark ground where the day's melting had begun and paused. He didn't notice the glow of a cell phone screen approaching him until it was well into the field. He'd been facing the other direction, expecting a car. But Cale snuck up on him.

Kate had arranged the reunion. Ambrose had heard her leave a voicemail message that was only "You will meet Ambrose in the field by the house tonight at nine. Delete this."

"Am," Cale said.

It was almost ten. "You're late," Ambrose said.

"An hour and almost a few decades, right?"

Ambrose had a rechargeable lantern in the duffel bag, but he didn't pull it out yet. "How's it going?"

"Fine. You?"

"Yeah, fine."

"Cold," Cale said.

"Yep." Ambrose had thought often over the years about what he would say to his brother if they ever spoke again, after so much time, so much silence. He'd thought their meeting would require an important speech to start. Some kind of acknowledgment of the obvious. But there was work to be done, so he just turned, and they moved toward the old path in the woods.

He glanced at Cale, who stepped a little gingerly in his leather loafers. He'd packed for a different sort of operation, clearly. His gear, a linen blazer and khaki slacks, was not appropriate for the venue or the job. Ambrose considered how his brother's attire might impact his plan. Cale had seemingly forgotten where he was from and how it was there.

At the bridge that their father had built over the brook, Ambrose turned on the lantern. They slid their feet over the damp mildewed boards, and then Cale followed him up a deer run through thick mountain laurel. The Casey plot was eight acres, and toward the back of it they came into a small clearing where Ambrose had already begun digging. Two shovels and a pickaxe leaned against an oak. They hadn't discussed any plan yet.

"You sure you want it here?" Cale asked.

"No," Ambrose said, and he stepped into the hole, which was only about knee deep. "Through the frost already." He began digging.

"You're thinking out in the open, then?"

"Thinking I don't want to spend hours cutting through pine roots."

Cale lifted the pickaxe and hacked at the head of the emerging grave, and they dug for a while without speaking, communicating only through the rhythm of the work. Sweating, his head steaming, Cale dropped the pickaxe and took off his blazer. He grabbed the other shovel. "So," he said. "Anything new?"

Ambrose stopped digging. He stared toward him. "What are you wearing?"

"Nice, right?"

"No." Ambrose went back to work.

"Look out, fashion police." Cale tried to keep it light. "We can't both look like tractor repairmen."

"I'm just wondering how soon before you quit, saying you're too cold."

"I'm fine."

"How soon before you quit?" he repeated.

Cale looked up at the moon. "You're pretty morose for a gravedigger."

"Get back to work. We're losing daylight here."

"Funny, I just flew across the world." Cale stabbed his shovel into the ground. "Don't you worry about me."

"We'll see."

An owl shrieked in the distance. A cool breeze whooshed through the trees and around them. Cale's shovel scraped against a rock and he worked the handle like a lever, pumping, prying it loose from the packed clay. He said, "I went to the office there in Nevin. Valley's."

Ambrose dropped his shovel. "Why?"

"Tried to make a deal."

"Why wouldn't you tell me before going?"

"Why?" Cale asked.

"You implicate us both," he said. "One hand can't not know what the other hand is doing."

"You haven't told me what you've been doing," Cale said.

"That's because you haven't been around."

"So, you got a plan for what happens after this, then, or you just want to rush in?"

"Got a plan." Ambrose spit.

"You think it can just be plucked out in one piece?"

"That comes next."

"We working hard here, Am, or are we working smart?"

"Shut up," he said, sounding as weary as he did dismissive.

"No, I'm not just gonna follow along now."

"It's too early to go over there," Ambrose said. "People are paying attention, even more now, thanks to you. We need a hole. You want to figure out where to put it on the back end? Maybe leave it out for a while, see what happens?"

"No, I don't want to do it at all."

Ambrose climbed out of the grave. "No shit," he said, in frustration, suppressing the volume. Then he paced in the moonlight with his hands on his head.

Cale continued to dig. When his brother came back over, he said, "I saw Lily Rowe."

"God dammit, Cale."

"She looks good."

Ambrose almost laughed, in surprise and disbelief.

"Yesterday night. I pulled into the Gibbses' driveway," Cale said. "I'm pretty sure her truck was there. I didn't stay."

"Hope they don't have cameras there, you goddamn fool."

Cale climbed out of the grave now too. "One other thing. On the topic of grievances."

"What else did you fuck up?"

"Hey now, Mister Perfect."

"Spit it out," Ambrose said.

"Fine." Cale took a deep breath. "Sorry I missed your wedding."

Ambrose laughed, releasing the tension. "That's a joke now?"

"Kind of. I mean, I mean it, but . . ."

"We invited you?"

"Kate insisted I be best man."

"Instead, you chose to be worst man."

"And boy, was I good, right?"

"No," Ambrose said. "Apology denied, but alright."

Cale laughed. They worked together in shifts for another hour, sweating through filthy shirts. The cold stuck to them, especially during the brief breaks. The lantern, on its dimmest setting, was kept down in the hole. When Ambrose went to take a leak or drink from the thermos he'd brought, the yellow light coming out of the ground made him think of mines being opened or the daylight coming through a window that was no longer boarded up. The sun unburied.

"Are you married?" Ambrose asked, giving Cale a hand as he climbed out of the hole. "Kids?"

"No," he said, with a sigh. "Some seeds shouldn't be replanted, right?" He laughed again, alone. "If I'm going to hell, I probably shouldn't drag anyone else along for the ride."

"You believe that?" Ambrose assessed the depth of the hole.

"Yes."

"You're religious?"

"Just that part of it," Cale said.

"The bad part."

"Right. That's all I've kept."

When it became increasingly difficult to get out of the grave, they agreed without a word that it was good enough. Ambrose climbed out once more and put on his jacket again. He turned off the lantern and they waited for their eyes to adjust. As kids, they'd run through those woods at night, no lights. Testing one another to go farther and farther from the house. To see who had more courage, less fear of coyotes, the dark.

They left the shovels and pickaxe leaning against a tree on the edge of the clearing and followed the deer run back down to the bridge. Instead of taking the old wagon trail up the hill to the house, they went along the brook until the path ended in a place of downed trees. Soon patches of skunk cabbage and fiddlehead ferns would begin to rise from that ground, but now there was still the thin snow over dead leaves in most places. They kept moving along the bank, knowing where the water led.

"You know if that tree Grandma carved is still there?" Cale asked.

"I never should've gone out there." Ambrose was thinking about Gibbs Pond. He was thinking about his wife, his daughter, the child on the way. They continued at an even clip. Where Apple Brook Road went over the water, they dropped down the bank and went under the bridge. The waterline was scattered with smooth dry stones the size of softballs, which tottered and knocked under their feet.

Cale asked what tools Ambrose had in the bag, but Ambrose didn't respond, lost in his thoughts. They continued to follow the brook through the sloping pasture, ducking their heads and moving at a brisk pace in the open sections between stands of trees. In this way, they reached the barbed wire fence that now hung slack. They went over it, onto what they'd known as the Gibbs property. At a small rise, the place where they'd once spoken with their father about Ray Rowe, they stopped, and Ambrose turned on the lantern again. He opened his bag. He had a handheld floodlight, too, a roll of garbage bags, a wetsuit that he'd bought that day with cash from the sporting goods store in Bellewood, and a thick yellow nylon rope to which he'd tied a makeshift grappling hook he'd fashioned from a rusty garden rake. He'd cut the head in half and soldered the halves together back-to-back. He was embarrassed by it.

"This is all you have?" Cale asked.

"What do you suggest?"

"Offer Gerlano more money?"

"I don't have it," Ambrose said. "And we don't have the time."

"Anything you hook and drag is just going to fall apart, like I said."

"Then it'll wash on downstream. A construction crew is coming in with heavy machinery. They're moving dirt, not running an archaeological dig with little brushes. There just can't be anything obvious. We can only do as much as we can, and hope we get lucky again."

"Lucky?" Cale laughed. "Give me the wetsuit."

"It's on me," Ambrose said.

"You have more to lose now than I do."

"I know."

"You know where it is?" Cale said.

"Yes." Ambrose sat down on the rise and grabbed the wetsuit. "We'll see how much it's moved." Checking the time, he glanced at his phone, which was set on silent mode. He saw he had four missed calls from Kate.

"You took that with you?" Cale said. "It tracks your location."

"This is weird," Ambrose said.

"I put mine in the crab apple tree."

"Something's off."

"Hey, kill the lantern," Cale whispered. He turned it off himself when Ambrose didn't. They got low, lying on their bellies. By Gibbs Pond, they saw a light moving around, aiming up into the trees and down, and then moving away from them, along the bank, until they lost sight of it. They waited, in near silence, trying to keep the sound of their breathing quiet, though both were panting.

"Who was that?" Cale asked. "It was moving all over."

"Security maybe? Would they have that?"

They sat in silence for a moment, listening. Cale said, "You didn't answer me when I asked if that tree Grandma carved is still there?"

Ambrose stared at his cell phone again.

"I've dreamt that we find her in the brook."

The screen lit up, Kate calling.

"Turn that off," Cale said.

"I can't." Ambrose slunk down the rise.

"What are you doing?" Cale hissed. "Stop."

Ambrose answered the call. Kate was crying. "Something's wrong."

"It's okay," he whispered. "We're almost done."

"With the baby," she said. "There's a lot of blood."

He felt faint. "Call an ambulance."

"I can't," she said. "They're gonna ask where you are."

25

Cale had almost no experience taking care of children, and suddenly he had Sadie. At dawn, trying to calm the screaming two-year-old, he felt a more profound anxiety than he had on his flight back into the past. More even than on the suddenly rushed mission to night dive in near-freezing waters for a corpse that had haunted him most of his life. He'd been gone from Macoun so long, returning had felt surreal. A movie in which he was merely playing a temporary part. Alien enough to carry a wisp of excitement, despite the real reason for being there.

But now he was holding the shrieking child, opening all the old kitchen cabinets and drawers he knew from before. Frenzied, he looked for anything to placate her. The last update he'd received from Ambrose, hours earlier, was that there'd been an emergency caesarean at the hospital. The baby, Cale didn't know the gender or the name, had been taken away to the neonatal intensive care unit. On the call, Ambrose failed to mask the terror in his voice.

The night before, the ambulance had arrived at the house only seconds after the brothers. They had run from the Gibbs property, up the steep road, and had cut into the field beside the Casey house when they heard the first siren approaching behind them, a ways off but moving fast. Ambrose went in through the door from the deck, took off his dirty shirt, and let the paramedics in through the garage. Panting and dazed, Cale found himself in the wobbling ambulance lights. A paramedic with wooden plugs for earrings looked him over and shook her head, clearly confused. Cale wondered if those piercings were against policy. Then he looked down at his slacks and shirt and loafers, all caked in dirt. His linen blazer wasn't as dirty as it was rumpled. Cale plucked a speck of lint from his sleeve. He shrugged. "Did some landscaping."

The paramedic raised her eyebrows and got into the driver's seat. Two more came out of the house and into the open garage with Kate on a gurney. A bloodstain was blooming on the white sheet that covered her legs and belly. She had an oxygen mask over her mouth and nose, but she glanced at him and said, in a sleepy way, "I thought you'd be taller." He could see, through the fog on the mask, the faintest smile. He was stunned, awed, by this first meeting.

Ambrose came out, a frantic look in his eyes. He'd put on a new sweatshirt, but his pants and boots were still covered in dirt. "You can stay here?"

"I can follow you there?"

"No, I need you to stay, I'm saying. Sadie's asleep." And then Ambrose climbed into the back of the ambulance and took his wife's hand. "I'll call when I can."

The paramedics shut the double doors. The ambulance was pulling out of the driveway by the time Cale managed to say, "What is she fed?" And then he was standing in the dark driveway, alone. He listened to the howl of the ambulance slowly diminish into silence. He heard the creaking of a single cricket and the faint drone of an airplane passing overhead. He turned to the house, and at a loss for what else to do, he just sat down in the driveway, until he remembered to go get his phone, which he'd tucked between a branch and the body of the crab apple tree in the field next door.

Later that night, he drifted through his childhood home, remembering how walls had been different colors, noticing the new couches, new pictures and curtains. It was all so deeply familiar and yet altered. In his midtwenties, what he considered his garbage years, he'd had an apartment in San Francisco, a bona fide roach motel, which had been broken into once and rifled through. The aspiring thieves, junkies no doubt, found nothing worth stealing, apparently. But what little he owned had been roughed up and tossed around carelessly in a way that made him shrink away from those objects forever after. Ambrose's house, that container of a happy childhood, gave him a similar feeling, albeit one of less violation. He wondered what it'd been like for his brother, all these years, living in it. Driving past Waquaheag Road, the Gibbses' house, the Gindewins', every day. Seeing the same faces in town, as he silently lied to them all. Letting them all go on thinking things that were not the truth, whether it was their business or not. The frequent reminders in plain sight constantly. Cale supposed that you sink into it, and it becomes like the old furniture, uncomfortable but comfortable in its familiarity after a while. It was perhaps the first time he'd contemplated his brother's pain, he realized, rather than solely his own and what'd happened to him. What he'd had to do to have his brother's back, as his father had told them. His selfishness struck him so suddenly he had to sit down again. It hit him like a club behind the knees. He wasn't the only sacrifice, he understood. They all were.

In the twilight, he texted Ambrose to see how they were doing, and then he stretched out on the couch and did something he hadn't done since he was a child. He prayed. He prayed with all he had, for Kate and the baby, and for his baby brother. His eyes clenched, the warm tears streaming from the seams. And just as he said "amen," in his way, and tried to relax and get some sleep, he heard Sadie crying upstairs.

He went up, each old stair creaking. His mouth dry, his heart inexplicably pounding. Slowly he opened the door to her bedroom, the slightly bigger one of the two upstairs, which had been Ambrose's. "Hi, Sadie. Nice to meet you finally. I'm your uncle Caleb. You can call me Cale."

Standing in the crib, she was quiet for a moment, before the crying resumed at double volume. He tried his best to soothe her.

"Hello, there. Hi. How are you?"

The screaming intensified.

"You're Sadie, right? Is your name Sadie?"

She did not relent.

"How about some breakfast? Are you hungry? Do you like smoothies? Does your dad have a blender?" He went over to the crib. She dropped to a seated position and rolled away from him. He turned on a table lamp and she bawled harder. He picked her up awkwardly, with her legs dangling, kicking. One foot hit him squarely in a testicle, and he lowered himself to the floor, feeling he might vomit. He thought about calling his mother for advice. Sadie was so loud, though, that he knew a call wouldn't work. He could barely hear himself, telling her nonsense in a futile attempt to calm her. "How about candy? You have any candy here you might like?"

He managed to get a firmer, gentler hold on her and stand. He carried her down the narrow wooden staircase, still hurting where she'd kicked him, the only upside of which was that it gave him a real pain to focus on in place of the fear that his fragile skull could pop. In the kitchen, a swell of panic rolled over the crown of his head and down his spine into his guts. His stomach bloated and his diaphragm tightened, affecting his ability to breathe. It would be a bad time to panic, he knew, which increased his sense of panic.

He strapped her into a high chair, hands trembling, and poured them both some orange juice in paper cups. He drank his first in the hope that it might stabilize his blood sugar or move his mind away from the state of a caged animal's. He set the cup of juice in front of her and she swatted it onto the floor and screamed. The juice soaked into the tan oval rug under the table. He sat in a chair across from her. Her face was red, cheeks slick with tears. He weighed his options, wondering what he could do, who he could call for help. There was no one. His legs felt weak. He felt it must be nature's way of preventing him from running away. To make him freeze, this time around, since he'd already fought and taken flight in other situations, and to what end?

"You know, it's been a stressful couple days," he said, with a sigh. "I didn't fully realize the toll this was taking on me. Maybe I didn't have time. Maybe it was too much time. I didn't sleep last night, so please don't make fun of me if I look less than presentable, okay, Sadie? You promise?"

Her crying softened.

"I'm worried about your family, in more ways than one. I'm worried about myself too, I guess, as always, in a way. That's been the story of my life, hasn't it? You know, I see how it happens. How people do it, you know, where you just can't take it and it's just too much. I was close a few times. So I know. But I'm glad I didn't do it, because look, here I am now meeting you."

The crying paused and she looked at him with a seeming glimmer of curiosity. Encouraged by the effect on them both, he continued. "I'm embarrassed. Generally, all the time, embarrassed. I've cut myself off from everyone. I thought that was for their sake, you know? But meanwhile, I was the one ignoring them. I pretended they didn't exist, because I didn't want to. And I tried to focus on tangible things, you know, surfaces, clothes. I tried to find some joy there. I wanted to be something different, something brand new, but I'm not and I never will be. Is that okay with you?"

She slapped the plastic tray of the high chair with both hands and started to cry again.

"Do you need a bottle?"

She shook her head no.

"I don't think I'm a diaper guy, nothing personal."

"Want orange," she said, garbling the word. "Orange juice."

"You promise you won't knock it over again?"

"Mama," she said. Her lip quivered. "Where's Mama?"

"I'll get the juice. She'll be right back, okay? She's tough. She'll be right back."

She closed her eyes and lifted her chin and the crying became a wail again. She knocked the new orange juice over when he brought it. After cleaning it up poorly, only putting paper towels on the stains and stepping on them, he said, "Should we take a ride in the car? That always calmed your dad down. I remember that."

He unstrapped her, still rattled himself, and carried her to the mudroom, where his parents had kept their car keys. He found the electronic openers for the truck and the minivan on the same hooks, and took them both. He got her purple puffy jacket in the closet and managed to get her hands through the proper sleeves and the rest of it in only about three arduous minutes. The crying, with its crescendos, jangled in his ears, but he was pleased to find a kid's car seat in the back of the truck. He wasn't ready for the minivan.

Sadie calmed down somewhat once he got her in the seat. He paused before opening the driver-side door and studied the script on it. It was almost the same as it'd been on their father's pickup. The day was cold, raw, clouds coming in fast, though the sun was high enough to illuminate the lettering. Despite the temperature, he could feel spring in the air, and pulling open the door, he remembered his father's story about the winds of home.

In the truck, they coasted down Apple Brook Road, the same way his dad had. The same way his brother had now almost all his life. They passed the bridge over the brook, and he knew where that led, and then they passed the sloping and rising pasture that he'd slunk across and sprinted through the night before. Approaching the Gibbses' old guesthouse, he glanced in the rearview mirror and saw Sadie calmly staring out the window. The sunlight slanting through the treetops on the east side of the road flickered across her face, and Cale had a strange feeling of disconnecting from himself. He felt suddenly relaxed and at the same time vaguely worried that he was losing his mind. That he'd lost his grip on some heavy and foundational anchor, and he was untethered like a balloon released to the breeze. Through the windshield, everything he saw suddenly felt vibrant and new, and without any meaning. Perhaps, he wondered later, that peculiar string of moments was why he didn't notice the Gibbses' house when he passed, or any activity in the driveway. And perhaps, he understood, without that image of Sadie staring calmly at most of the same things that he had at her age, he likely would not have turned up Waquaheag Road without a thought.

Nearing Seb Bainer's field, he looked again at his niece in the rearview mirror, reminding his body that he could not jerk the steering wheel now and relive a destiny that was not his, or at least not hers. On the road shoulder, he saw an old man, bent so far forward that his back was at a forty-five-degree angle to the ground. It looked as if he were battling a gale wind. He was standing near where the tree had been, the one Seb had cut down after the accident. As he slowed, Cale wasn't sure it was Seb at first. In fact, he was surprised to learn that Seb was still alive at all. The old man turned to the truck. Cale leaned over, manually rolling down the passenger-side window.

"Ambrose," Seb said, his voice thin and raspy. He wore a red-and-black-checked flannel hat. He had a Band-Aid on his forehead, and his corduroy pants and canvas barn coat billowed around him.

"Hey, Seb. It's actually Cale. Ambrose's brother. Driving his truck."

Seb nodded and turned away again, looking at the ground. "More snow coming today."

"It's been a while," Cale said. "How you doing?"

Seb shrugged and then slowly bent farther to pick something up from the ground. He let out a faint groan doing so, and when he stood, Cale saw that he held a pale white stick. Birch. "Don't know how this got here," he said. "Wind, must've been."

Cale nodded, watching Seb examine the little limb.

He turned it over in his trembling hands. "Look like a bone, don't it?"

Cale leaned back in his seat. "Whose?" he wondered aloud, recalling his dream. Maybe it hadn't been about the death of his father or Ray, but rather his own.

Through the windshield, he saw a black pickup truck pull out of the Rowes' driveway and turn onto the road toward him, the same truck he'd seen already. It was Lily's, he knew. His phone vibrated in his pocket. He took it out and answered Ambrose's call.

"How's it going, Am?"

"We're good," he said, with enough relief in his voice for Cale to believe it. "Baby's with Kate now. Baby's good. Kate's good."

"Thank God," Cale said as the black truck approached and slowed.

Ambrose laughed, exhausted. "How's Sadie?"

"She's good. I've got it."

"Thanks." And before Cale could ask what the baby's name was, Ambrose said, "Let's just leave it alone, you know? What could we ever have even done anyway?"

"You alright?" Cale asked, understanding with sudden clarity the right thing to do. It was on him. He acted alone, he'd say. It was that simple. The reckoning, but not at the cost of these kids, too.

"In most ways, yes," Ambrose said.

"Okay," Cale said, watching Seb move toward the oncoming truck. And before he could ask again about the baby, Ambrose said, "Kate got a strange message from Joan. Can you go check on her?"

26

Joan was in bed looking through some folders she'd taken from Harvey's study. She had no expectation of discovering anything new. The warping of time, she felt, would not shed new light on the events they couldn't understand when the wounds had been new. But she hoped that the effort would mean something to Harvey. That perhaps the shared mission could bring him back to her, out of the hinterlands, out of his dreams. She wanted him to focus on his exercises and the life all around them still. So far, he hadn't listened. As she was trying to reach him, sifting through his memories, she came upon a manila envelope labeled *Rose*. It caught her by surprise and took her breath away. When she opened it, she found it was the first draft of Harvey's book that'd been interrupted. She didn't know that he'd written that much. It had no title, no name. On the dedication page, where he should've honored their daughter, he'd written that the book was for Joan. She got only as far that night as the first page, which explained that he couldn't write a history of the town, but the best he could attempt was a history of his family there, of his love in that place.

She stopped when she heard Harvey downstairs. That wasn't unusual, but something compelled her then to get up and go to him. In the kitchen, he had the old long-handled Maglite he'd carried in his cruiser for years. When he saw her in the doorway, he looked down at the floor with a faint nod, acknowledging, she felt, something beyond understanding. He went over and kissed her forehead, put his hand to her cheek. It was a small gesture, but she realized it was his tenderness that she'd missed most. The stroke had taken more than just his words. But it seemed like he was coming back to her, in some way, finally. He slipped a folded index card into the pocket of her cardigan, and then he turned to the door.

"Goodbye," she said. "I love you."

He nodded and put his hand to his heart. He blew her a kiss, then he went out the door. There was no stopping him, she knew. No stopping it. And she let him go.

Days later, she wondered how much of it was her fault, as she sat on her back deck, looking down at a forsythia bush that'd begun to bud. Soon it would be bursting with yellow flowers and birds. The bush told her that the hard frosts were likely over for the year, though that wouldn't make it any easier for the excavator in the cemetery yet. She tried to think instead about what else the buds told her. A new season had come or was coming, and soon enough it'd be time to prune the roses.

"I don't think I'll do that this year, though," she said. The sun was bright. The sky a deep cloudless blue. It was a Tuesday, and warm, the kind of day when people in town cheerfully told one another that spring had indeed sprung. Joan wore a black puffy winter jacket with a patch of duct tape on the sleeve. She was having chardonnay and crackers for lunch.

"What's that now?" Kate Casey sat beside her in a matching wicker rocker, looking down at the new baby, not yet four days old, bundled against her, sleeping. She'd left the hospital as soon as she could. She'd stayed longer when Sadie was born, but that was before the pandemic and the protocols and timings had changed. And she didn't like being there anyway. Plus, she needed to go see Joan. It was the day she'd come every week since Harvey's stroke, and it was important to her to keep the date, especially now.

"The roses," Joan said. "It's a lot of work."

"I can help."

"You've got your hands full."

"I got two hands full. Between you and me, though, we have four hands."

"That's nice," she said. "How're you feeling?"

"Pretty good, all things considered," Kate said. "Gotta move slow and take it easy. Keep walking."

"Isn't that just amazing," Joan said.

"We got lucky."

"For all the bad, some things do get better, don't they?" Joan rocked in the chair, studying the rest of the yard. "Maybe I'll go stay with my sister for a while. It's been four or five years. I've got grandnieces I haven't even met yet. When she gets here, maybe I'll ask."

"Sounds like a good plan."

Joan stared at her. "Why'd you take those papers from Harvey, anyway?"

Kate's face took on a stricken expression. She paused, thinking. "I was trying to figure out, you know, that test."

Joan rocked. "Believe me, I've read about a lot of tests. I talked to a lot of people about a lot of ways of getting him back."

"I know you have," Kate said. Their eyes met, and Kate looked away. "You ever feel like you were married to a stranger?"

"No." Joan shook her head definitively. Then, "Well, maybe a little, in the end. But no."

"It couldn't have been easy."

"Nothing is."

Kate shifted the baby.

"Harvey, Harvey, Harvey," Joan said. "Just couldn't stop blaming himself. Those kids long grown, and he's still carrying it all those years."

"A good man."

Joan got up slowly and opened the storm door, still glass instead of a screen. "You take good care of little Eli now."

Kate turned to her. "I didn't tell you his middle name yet."

"That's okay."

"Eli Harvey Casey."

Joan nodded. "On and on we go, right?"

It was clearly not the response Kate had expected. But Joan didn't have the energy or desire to say anything further. She went inside, and the spring-hinged storm door slammed behind her. She shut the wood door inside and slid the deadbolt, locking it. In the kitchen, she dumped her wine in the sink and put the glass on the counter. The wake was coming and she still had to get the house ready for her sister and the nieces and the children who were on their way. She had to get herself ready too.

She glanced at a copy of the *Hartford Courant* on the counter. They'd run a human-interest piece on Harvey and his career. The framing of it, the story of the rose house, was only a little sappy, she felt, and they didn't hammer too hard on the obvious beauty-and-thorn stuff. Joan supplied a picture of Harvey in uniform standing by one of the bushes in June of 1988.

When the journalist, a woman named Leslie Diaz, stopped by and introduced herself and her intention, Joan said, "I didn't think you existed anymore." The journalist laughed and then stopped laughing when she saw Joan was serious and more accurate than not. "What you should really tell about," Joan said, "is Valley Development and what they're doing next door. It doesn't seem right, and I'm not done with it." She went on to tell the story of Meryl Gibbs, and her son selling the land, and the sneaky approach of the developer. "No one will care," Joan said, "but I will. And Harvey would, too, I know it."

"I'll dig in."

"Good," Joan said. "The lawyers will beat me easily, I'm sure, but that doesn't mean people shouldn't know what happened, because it happens everywhere. These exploiters just take and take."

"I don't mean to intrude, but why was your husband there?" she said, jotting down notes the old-fashioned way, on a reporter's pad.

Harvey had been found against a big maple on the bank of Gibbs Pond by a construction worker who thought, he told the police, that he'd just come upon somebody sleeping. He didn't want to wake him, he said, because he seemed so peaceful. Harvey didn't fall or drown, as Joan had gotten tired of warning him he might. Though his shoes and pants were wet, as if he'd been wading knee-deep in the water. The exact cause of death was still unknown, pending lab results. Another stroke was the likely candidate, but Joan didn't want to know. She just wanted to picture him there, taking a snooze, as if it had been one of those summer days when they were first married, when they'd gone down to that pool to picnic and swim. Sometimes they met Meryl Gibbs and her boyfriend, Tom, long gone now, the rolling-stone father of the son who sold the family land. Meryl would bring a thermos of mixed Manhattans and they'd catch trout that Joan and Harvey would take home to wrap in foil with lemon and cook on the charcoal barbecue. Glass of wine on the deck as the sun went down on the backyard that was still all just woods.

Joan couldn't explain to the journalist exactly why Harvey had gone to Gibbs Pond that night, his last. She said that he didn't think it was right what they were doing there. Something was off. She said that, as a cop, Harvey was a man of principle and a protector, and he wanted to preserve the land. That detail didn't make it into the puff piece. But the journalist said to expect at least one follow-up story, if not more.

Joan put the newspaper in the recycling, then washed and dried her wineglass. Through the window, she saw Ambrose and Sadie playing catch in the front yard with an old tennis ball. The day before, the other Casey boy had stopped by to bring flowers. Joan gave him the note that Harvey had tucked into her sweater pocket before he left that night. She didn't know why she'd done that, an impulse, but she felt that message hadn't been for her. Harvey's messages were all around, and just because it was the last one, she didn't believe that made it the most important.

Cale had asked if there was anything he could do for her, so she gave it to him and said, "Yeah, get rid of this." He read it and left, and then he sat in his car in the driveway staring at it for what seemed like a long time to her, too long. Only a handful of minutes probably, but she wanted to be alone. He didn't leave until she went out and asked if everything was okay.

And now she watched his brother, greeted by his wife, who'd gone around the house to leave, understanding, it seemed, that there was nothing more to say between them. No goodbyes. She watched that family put the kids in their truck. Ambrose saw her through the window and waved, but she stepped back from view. She'd spent the night looking through more of Harvey's papers and she thought she knew now what had happened, though she wondered how Ambrose and his brother could've done it. Just children, capable of such violence. They'd killed Abe Rowe, she thought, and disposed of his body so well that even Harvey couldn't find it in thirty years of looking. Abe must have played a part in Eli Casey's death, and she wondered how quickly thereafter his sons had taken their revenge. How could seemingly good boys be so cold and calculating? Sunday-schooled and yet committing the gravest sin. Maybe it was shock, or something else entirely, in the water, in the times? And she understood that those answers would be among the many she'd never get in this life. You don't know some people, and then you do, and then you don't.

27

Lily felt Cale watching her in the church. She glanced back twice with the intention of making him stop. But each time she felt something waver and she understood that her message was not clear. Because she wasn't sure.

She'd seen him in his brother's truck talking to Seb Bainer, just down the street from her house. Thinking it was Ambrose again, come to beg about a minor job, she'd prepared to yell at him, regardless of what her family had done to his. His half-cocked arrivals at night had startled and confused her, and now she was sure he'd sabotaged Joe Wheeler's equipment. Not that she cared about Joe. Replacing him proved to be the right move. But Ambrose had interfered with her plans, with her work, and that pissed her off on principle. The guy just couldn't see the big picture, she thought. She'd gone years at a time without speaking to him, and suddenly he was everywhere. But when she pulled up beside the truck, she saw Cale, and any coarse words she had in mind left her. She went blank and drove on without even a wave. Ten seconds down the road, she got the call from the contractor she'd hired out of Massachusetts, an off-the-books deal. He told her they'd found a body, but he hadn't contacted the police yet. She felt that this discretion was a good sign for him. Her immediate instinct was to go into problem-solving mode.

"Let me get in touch with our head of comms," she said. "And legal."

"Okay. What do you want us to do in the meantime?"

"What're you doing now?"

"Still kinda working a little, to be honest."

"I'm not stopping you." She prepared to hang up.

"We were well underway when one of the guys noticed a flashlight in the water, and when he looked up the bank, there he was. It was bizarre."

She slowed down in her truck. "Wait, what's he look like?"

"Looks like an old man taking a nap. Scar down his cheek."

"Call the police." She hung up. She pulled over at the bottom of Waquaheag Road and put her head in her hands, and she began to sob for the first time since her own father had died, but with more pure sadness. She'd cried for Ray in the days after he left her, but she understood he had to go. One conversation with the cops about Eli Casey, and they would've sniffed Ray out. He didn't have her savvy, even if he lacked her remorse. The storm, with the frenzy and disruption of it, had created the opportunity he needed to escape, and she'd stopped resenting him for not saying goodbye. She understood now that he'd probably been worried she would beg to go with him, and somebody had to stay to look after their mother.

As for Harvey, she'd known him since her family came to town. He'd been the first person to come check on them. And then he'd been the one to whom she would confess. But no more, and she knew too, for reasons related and unrelated, that she would resign from her job that day. She didn't know what came next, for the first time since she was a child, and she didn't care.

Later, she knew Cale would come to her after the funeral, though they'd had no contact outside of her sparing glances. She waited for him on the front steps of her house, leaning against the cracked railing with a cup of coffee. It was a Thursday afternoon, St. Patrick's Day, though that meant little to her. The weather was warm, with that spring quality of surging. Of daylilies and daffodils gathering their strength to thrust up through the soft ground. In the thicket along the yard, the birds squeaked and squabbled with added fervor. She picked out the trilling call of a cardinal, her favorite. The year before, a pair of them had made a nest in a bush outside her bedroom window. She'd watched them build it and noted the arrival of the eggs. They seemed to signal good luck. The fledglings, though, were torn apart by starlings, and it only made her love them more. Now she saw a flit of red as a male disappeared into a hemlock, and then the tan female, and she thought that it was probably the same birds, and that this year they'd try again. She wondered if, in their bird brains, they remembered what had happened, and whether that was good or bad or both.

The morning after Eli Casey crashed, she was sitting out there on that same little porch, listening to the birds. She'd seen Ray drive off in their father's truck the day before, and she was feeling abandoned, when he came out of the woods. She ran to him, but stopped short of hugging him. He told her that he'd ditched the truck to throw off the cops, and that she'd have to use her smarts to come up with another way for them to get the hell out of there. And then they sat together, not saying a word, just listening.

Waiting for Cale, it occurred to her that of all her time alone, of which there'd been plenty, sitting on the steps with a coffee and the birds was probably her favorite thing to do. She wondered if having another person there to share that with would make it better or not, and decided that the answer was probably no, unless it was Ray. The Ray she remembered from before they'd come to this town, when it was them against the world. It was here, she felt, that their bond had given way, perhaps as a matter of age or growing up, at least the way they had grown up. On the Internet, she'd looked for him often and everywhere. Not that he'd be the type to waste his time pissing into the digital vacuum, as she thought of it. But there were no arrest write-ups or anything else that she could find. She called people in the places they'd lived before, even old Mr.

Figlio, but Ray hadn't backtracked, it seemed. No one had seen or heard from him. It left her to assume that he was out there, somewhere the wilderness remained, hunting and trapping by now.

She went inside to get a second mug of coffee and when she came back out, Cale was pulling in, in the blue sedan she'd seen in the parking lot at work. The same one, she suspected, that'd shown up in the Gibbses' driveway when she was waiting for Daniel, and waiting for Harvey, and as always, waiting for Ray. Without breaking stride, she stepped off the porch and brought the coffee to his car window. She'd just known he was coming. That same seemingly supernatural intuition. There was no explaining it. She just felt things, knew them way down deep sometimes, somehow.

"Hope you like it black," she said.

"This is for me?" He took the coffee through the open window, stammering. "How'd you know?"

"Maybe you stalking me in the church and the cemetery tipped me off."

"Sorry," he said. "I just couldn't take my eyes off you. Still, after all this time."

"Well, you should," she said. "Because it'll never happen, no matter what." She waited for him to protest. She'd had a few suitors before, not all losers, and she'd learned the importance of being blunt and stomping out any ambiguity around their hopes. It seemed harsh at first, and she'd been called a bitch by a few assholes, but it was more humane really, in the end, she felt. It saved everyone time, the most important resource. To her surprise, though, he just nodded sadly and said, "I know."

"You do?"

"Yeah."

"So why are you here?"

"I'm supposed to leave tomorrow," he said. "Scheduled to, anyway. We didn't get a chance to have dinner or drinks."

She raised her coffee and her eyebrows.

"Right," he said. "So I guess I just wanted to say hello, and goodbye."

"Okay." She sat on the hood of his car. He got out and it struck her again how much he looked like his father. He was about as old as his father had ever been. They were about the same height, same build, almost the same face. It pained her, knowing what she alone knew, she and Ray. Though she felt, too, that whatever story Cale told himself about what had happened, it was probably better than knowing what really did. For him, she determined, it was best to think of it all as just an accident. It wouldn't help him to know that his father had run scared from a boy, whom she was still protecting. Still, she'd lost her confidence and the upper hand she felt she'd had upon his predicted arrival. Now she didn't want to look at him. She was afraid he'd see the truth somehow.

"Do you remember when I told you I loved you?" He shook his head, laughing.

"No," she said. "That wasn't you."

They drank the coffee in silence for a while, until he nodded and stuck his chin forward. "Your brother," he said, as if something was stuck in his throat. "I'm sorry." Cale made a strange gurgling sound, and he heaved like he might vomit, as she remembered his brother had.

She slid off the hood and took a step away, noticing the tears in his eyes, the quivering face. She felt her own chin trembling, despite her efforts to remain strong.

"Sorry." He held up his fist to his mouth and took a breath. "It was my fault. It's your right to know."

Her heart pounded. "I don't know what you're talking about."

"He died." Cale nodded, seemingly regaining his resolve. "I'm so sorry. And I plan to turn myself in and take responsibility for what happened. For the accident."

She threw her coffee in his face. It wasn't hot enough to scald him, but he winced and remained silent, his eyes closed. She said, "Don't you ever talk about my brother again, you got it? You sick piece of shit."

"I am that," he said, wiping his eyes. "But when you dredge Gibbs Pond, you'll find him. The words aren't enough, I know. Hopefully, it gives you some peace that I'll pay for it now, not that I haven't most of my life."

"Stop," she commanded him.

"I'm just telling you."

"The pond was already dredged."

His mouth hung open. "It was?"

"And there was nothing, just the mud and sticks and shit."

"I came to tell you the truth," he said. "That's it."

"You didn't tell me anything," she said in a voice of quiet power. Her eyes burned. "Now I'm going into the house to get a knife. And if you aren't gone when I come out, I'm going to stab you with it as many fucking times as I can." She turned and moved quickly toward the house, tossing her coffee cup into the yard. She pushed the front door open hard and went to the drawer where she kept the knife. She grabbed it, but then went into the living room, unsure of her intentions. When she came out, his car was pulling out of the driveway slowly, with none of the urgency his father had shown when he ran from Ray. She threw the knife toward him, but it curved and landed well short in the yard.

On the cracked railing, he'd left the mug she'd brought him, and underneath it was a creased index card that'd been unfolded. She threw the extra mug at his car too. It tumbled silently on the lawn and the handle broke off. She looked at the index card and recognized the writing on it from when Harvey had shown up in her yard that day with a note just like it. She spit and crumpled it up and cast it aside like a piece of trash. The note slid slightly across a patch of ice crust in a warm breeze, and she went back into the house she'd almost fixed and made right entirely.

When the rain fell and the thaw continued, she saw the note's ink became illegible, a mottled bruise. The paper disintegrated into a white glob, and soon it became nothing more than dirt. She thought about it later, as she considered her father's bones moldering in that same dirt, as she continued her vigil for Ray. The two of them, the only people alive, in her mind, who knew why it'd all ended for Eli Casey, though Harvey Gindewin, she felt, had somehow come to know it in his final days. Still, his note meant nothing to her, and she felt it never would.

28

The Casey brothers went out into those woods one last time together, a couple of days after Harvey's funeral. They had to fill in the unused grave, on the slim chance some lost hiker happened upon it, Cale said, or a deer fell in and broke its leg. And when Ambrose asked if it was against the law to dig a hole on your own property, Cale insisted that they at least had to go get the tools they'd left there. On the way out, as he followed Ambrose up the deer run again, Cale let his brother know what he'd told Lily Rowe.

Ambrose didn't turn around or say anything, but his whole body seemed to stiffen and then sag, and his steps through the leaf litter slowed. He didn't ask Cale why he'd done that. But as they entered the clearing, Ambrose was struck once more by his brother's selfishness. They'd spoken about the danger of one hand not knowing what the other one was doing, and here he'd gone and done it again.

They'd been spared. Somehow, a grace had been given, and Cale could not just accept that for what it was.

"I know what you're thinking," Cale said. "But it wasn't for me that I felt I had to do that. It was for her."

Ambrose turned and snapped at him. "Why do you care more about her than your own family?"

Cale looked hurt. "It was for you too."

"I feel like we dodged a bullet somehow, and you decided, without my knowledge or okay, that you'd just pull us all back in front of it again. And not just me, Kate and the kids too."

"I'm not going to do that," he said. "I'm going to turn myself in. I acted alone, Am. It was me who did it. That's it. End of story."

Ambrose turned and stomped off. "What's that gonna do now, huh? Don't be a goddamn idiot."

"I understand," Cale said, remaining calm, almost at ease. "It's been easier for me because I left. But you still have to go on living here, seeing these people, including her."

Ambrose almost laughed. "Who said I do?" He went over to the tree where they'd left their tools. "Maybe we won't. Maybe I'm done with this place too, like I should've been." The wooden handles of the old shovels and pickaxe were damp and slick. "You do what you're gonna do, Cale. I can't change that." He grabbed a shovel and flung it in his brother's direction. It spun in circles through the air and landed between them. Ambrose went over to the pit. He looked down at the puddle in it. He didn't remember the night's rain, but his boots and the shins of his jeans were wet from walking through the underbrush. He'd slept well, deeply, for the first night in many years, and the baby hadn't woken him or even Kate too much. He was a good sleeper and eater so far, little Eli. Poor Sadie had been colicky and woke up shrieking like a wet cat many times a night for months. Ambrose smiled to himself, thinking about them for a moment, before his mood shifted again.

Cale picked up the shovel. The mounds of dirt along the hole were packed down from the rain. "She didn't believe me," he said.

"Good."

"And that doesn't mean she won't believe me once she has time to process it, but I don't know. Seemed like she had her mind pretty made up. Seems like she's the kind of person who can really make up her mind. Probably always had to."

Ambrose looked at him seriously. "Maybe she'll try to kill you."

Cale blinked. Bewilderment crossed his face. "I hadn't thought of that."

Ambrose laughed.

"That's funny?"

"I'm laughing because it's ridiculous, but true," he said.

"She did throw a knife at me."

"See."

"And a coffee cup."

"I wish she had better aim," Ambrose said.

"You think her dad had something to do with ours?" Cale said. "I wanted to ask her, but then she threatened to stab me. Didn't seem like the best time."

"Probably," Ambrose said. "I'm sure he got what was coming to him one way or another by now, wherever he is, right?"

Cale jammed his shovel into the dirt mound. "My back's still hurting from the last time we dug this."

"Fuck it anyway," Ambrose said. "I'll say I tried to dig a pond."

"What about the deer?"

"You can't save them all, can you?"

"But what if a charismatic young porcupine accidentally topples in?"

"I never liked porcupines, even the charismatic ones."

"Remember when Sammy got hit by one?"

"Maybe that's why."

They started to walk back, the tools split between them. Cale said, "By the way, I got a voicemail this morning from your guy over at Valley Development."

"Gerlano?"

"He kept my business card after all."

"So?"

"He said he might consider discussing the sale of the Gibbs property after all, but he'd have to account for the value his development would bring to it."

"So he'd sell?"

"Negotiate anyway. Bad press, maybe?"

"Overextended too," Ambrose said. "At Harvey's thing, Joe Wheeler told me Lily quit. She was their workhorse."

"Hm," Cale said. "So, what do you think?"

"Pass," Ambrose said, of the land he'd wanted for most of his life. "You gonna do that deal from prison?"

Cale considered that as they crossed the bridge their father had built over the brook. "Should we go see Grandma's tree, while we can?"

"Either it's still there or it's not," Ambrose said. "Let's go see the kids."

Cale had already checked out of his hotel in Nevin, and he spent the night at Ambrose's, in his childhood home, in the bedroom that'd been his. They held a belated birthday celebration for their father, who would've been seventy-two. He was born on March 5, 1950, and died a week after he turned forty-three.

"I'm older now than he ever was," Cale said, as together he and his brother made their father's favorite meal, spaghetti and meatballs. "But I know so much less than he did."

"Like what?"

"Like the way he grew up. He could've turned into a terrible person, like me, but he didn't. He was tougher than that. There was something else in him, something better."

"You're not that bad, brother."

"I'm not that good either."

Ambrose poured dry pasta into a pot of boiling water. "Well, it's fine to be okay, right?"

Cale laughed. "That's my best chance, I think."

"You figured something out he didn't, though."

"How's that?"

"You're rich now, right?" Ambrose asked.

"I don't feel like it."

"It's amazing how you just get reduced to numbers, in the end."

"Yeah," Cale said, glancing at Ambrose's family on the couch in the kitchen. Kate held the new baby in one arm as she turned the page of a book with her free hand, reading to Sadie. "I don't know."

The next morning, they all waved goodbye as Cale pulled out of the driveway. When the car disappeared down Apple Brook Road, Ambrose turned back to the house. The same one he'd lived in all his life, while his brother had gone out and seen the world. He knew then that he'd sell it, and they'd move wherever Kate wanted to go. Wherever the schools were good, maybe near the beach. Somewhere he could take the kids fishing, deep sea.

Cale watched the rearview mirror until the road bent. He was booked on a flight in two hours to cross the world again, but he missed the turn along the way and kept driving toward Route 44. He'd had second thoughts about turning himself in, and he had the idea of going to see his mother. But he was thinking then about Harvey's note. For some reason, it'd gone from Harvey to Joan to Cale, and he in turn had given it away. Turning off Apple Brook Road, he wondered what Harvey had meant by it and for whom he had written it. It felt true in some way, but Cale couldn't say yet whether it was. It read only—the past isn't gone, it's just not here anymore. You are forgiven.

Acknowledgments

Many thanks to many, especially my family: Flash and Wange; Liz, Wyatt, and Pete; Ethan, Jamie, Luke, and their better halves and broods; Michael and Kathie Fox, the JJ Foxes, and Foxes everywhere; John, Marilyn, and all the SteinStoreySztybels.

Thanks to my agent, Duvall Osteen, and to Nicole Aragi and the ARAGI team.

Thanks to my editor, Joe Brosnan, and to Morgan Entrekin and everyone at Grove Atlantic who helped bring this thing to life.

Thanks to my best teachers, in particular: Denis, Xuefei, Sigrid, Leslie, and Ada.

Thanks to Boston University and Washington University in St. Louis.

Thanks to Ted Thompson.

Thanks to my friends, whose names I will omit for brevity.

And thanks to you, whomever is reading this. Your time is precious. Thank you.